SUPER SLEUTH

David Walliams

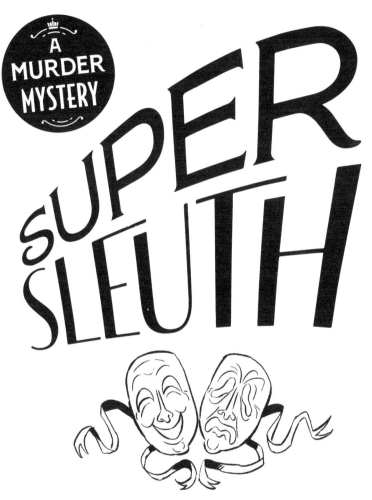

A MURDER MYSTERY

SUPER SLEUTH

ILLUSTRATED BY **ADAM STOWER**

HC CB

HARPERCOLLINS CHILDREN'S BOOKS

First published in the United Kingdom by
HarperCollins *Children's Books* in 2024
HarperCollins *Children's Books* is a division of HarperCollins*Publishers* Ltd
1 London Bridge Street
London SE1 9GF

www.harpercollins.co.uk

HarperCollins*Publishers*
Macken House, 39/40 Mayor Street Upper
Dublin 1, D01 C9W8, Ireland

1

HB ISBN 978-0-00-830585-7
TPB ISBN 978-0-00-861451-5
PB ISBN 978-0-00-861443-0

David Walliams and Adam Stower assert the moral right to be identified
as the author and illustrator of the work respectively.

This is a work of fiction. Names, characters, businesses, places, events, locales and
incidents are either the products of the author's imagination or used in a fictitious
manner. Apart from famous historical figures, any resemblance to actual persons,
living or dead, or actual events is purely coincidental.

A CIP catalogue record for this title is available from the British Library.

Printed and bound in the UK using 100% renewable electricity
at CPI Group (UK) Ltd

Conditions of Sale

This book is produced from independently certified FSC™ paper
to ensure responsible forest management.

For more information visit: www.harpercollins.co.uk/green

For Wylda and Romy.

Two supercool cats.

THE SCENE WAS SET FOR MURDER:

An ocean liner.

The world's greatest detective on board.

And over a thousand crew and passengers.

One of them a murderer...

OUR CAST OF CHARACTERS:
THE PASSENGERS

LORD FOX
Gladys's dashing aristocratic suitor.

AUNTIE GLADYS
Dilly's aunt hates children, and Dilly in particular.

DILLY
Dilly loves detective stories. Her dream is that one day she will be a super sleuth herself.

WATSON
Dilly's best friend in the whole world is also her assistant in sleuthing.

THE PROFESSOR
A Hungarian scientist.

THE BRIGADIER
A red-nosed, one-armed old soldier.

MOROSOV
An intense and brooding Russian novelist.

THE BLACK WIDOW
An elderly Norwegian lady.

MAGNUS MAGNUS
An Icelandic composer.

THE CREW

THE CAPTAIN
A no-nonsense, ex-navy officer who has a secret soft side.

CHEF
A highly strung Turkish chef.

THE MAÎTRE D'
The snobby French king of the restaurant.

HUNTER
The rough, tough, gruff Scottish engine-room worker.

THE SETTING

THE MASQUERADE

The finest ocean liner in the world.
Wondrous. Glamorous. Luxurious.
THE MASQUERADE crosses the Atlantic Ocean
from England to America in just one week.

FUNNELS

PORTHOLES

UNION
JACK

PROMENADE

GIANT PROPELLERS

CROW'S NEST

BRONZE BUST OF POSEIDON, THE GREEK GOD OF THE SEA

BRIDGE

LIFEBOATS

DECK

THE 1920s

They were called the Roaring Twenties. No wonder: there was an explosion of jazz music, dance crazes and exciting movies. It was a thrilling time to be alive. So it's a shame that on board **THE MASQUERADE** so many would end up dead.

PROLOGUE

Dilly loved a good murder.

Not a real murder.

No.

A made-up murder.

One you would find in a murder-mystery novel.

Dilly adored detective stories. This was something she had inherited from her father, who had left behind a huge collection of books. She'd devoured every single one before finding more and more in the local library.

Sherlock Holmes stories were her favourite – so much so that she had named her dog Watson after the master detective's faithful companion. Dilly had trained her Watson to sniff

out clues and follow scent trails – something he would happily do for a dog biscuit. Or two.

"RUFF!"

EXHIBIT: **DILLY**

WILD HAIR

GLASSES

JUMPER

TORN
DUFFEL
COAT

DIRTY
HANDS

SCRATCHES ON
KNEES

MUDDY SHORTS

LONG
WOOLLEN
SOCKS (ODD)

WATSON

BOOTS WITH HOLES

A STUDY IN SCARLET

The SIGN of the FOUR

The VALLEY of FEAR

The HOUND of the BASKERVILLES

The Adventures of SHERLOCK HOLMES

THE MEMOIRS OF SHERLOCK HOLMES

The Return of Sherlock Holmes

SHERLOCK HOLMES: HIS LAST BOW

THE CASEBOOK of SHERLOCK HOLMES

The BIG FOUR

THE MYSTERY OF THE BLUE TRAIN

The Thirty-nine Steps

SPEEDY DEATH

The RED HOUSE MYSTERY

The GREENE MURDER CASE

Whose Body?

THE BENSON MURDER CASE

The House without a key

ALIAS THE LONE WOLF

The MURDER ON THE LINKS

POIROT INVESTIGATES

The Murder of ROGER ACKROYD

Dilly travelled everywhere with her battered old school satchel.

EXHIBIT: **DILLY'S DETECTIVE KIT**

MAGNIFYING GLASS

NOTEBOOK

DOG BISCUITS

PENCIL

SPARE PENCIL

SPARE, SPARE PENCIL

BOX OF MATCHES

CANDLE

CHALK (FOR TRACING ROUND A DEAD BODY)

SMALL SQUARE OF FUDGE (TO BE UNWRAPPED ONLY IN AN EMERGENCY)

PAPERCLIP TO PICK LOCKS

EVIDENCE BAGS AND TAGS

Despite Dilly placing a card in the window of her local post office…

PRIVATE DETECTIVE FOR HIRE

SPECIALISES IN MURDER, BUT WILL CRACK ANY CASE

PAYMENT CAN BE MADE IN FUDGE*

AND DOG BISCUITS

* IF THE CASE IS NOT CRACKED, THERE IS A FUDGE-BACK GUARANTEE.

...there hadn't been many takers so far beyond:

Old Ma Evans, whose cat had mysteriously disappeared from the village. It turned out she had accidentally locked Teacake in a cupboard.

The local vicar, who reported a Custard Cream biscuit stolen from the vicarage. He'd forgotten that he'd eaten it.

The farmer, who reported that one of his flock of sheep had gone missing. It wasn't missing at all. He just couldn't count to twelve.

But now the detective duo found themselves on a transatlantic liner.

The perfect place for a murder.

Or two.

Or three.

Or four.

Or more...

ACT I

DEATH BY BLANCMANGE

CHAPTER ONE
A WHIRLWIND

New York was spectacular at night: the skyscrapers competing to reach the stars, the Brooklyn Bridge stretching over the East River, and the Statue of Liberty presiding over it all like a goddess.

Families and friends gathered on the dock, waving goodbye to their loved ones on board the mighty MASQUERADE. The ship was a floating five-star hotel. The mightiest cruise liner the world had ever seen. It took passengers at record speed across the Atlantic Ocean. Just one week to travel three thousand miles.

EXHIBIT: **CROSS-SECTION OF THE MASQUERADE**

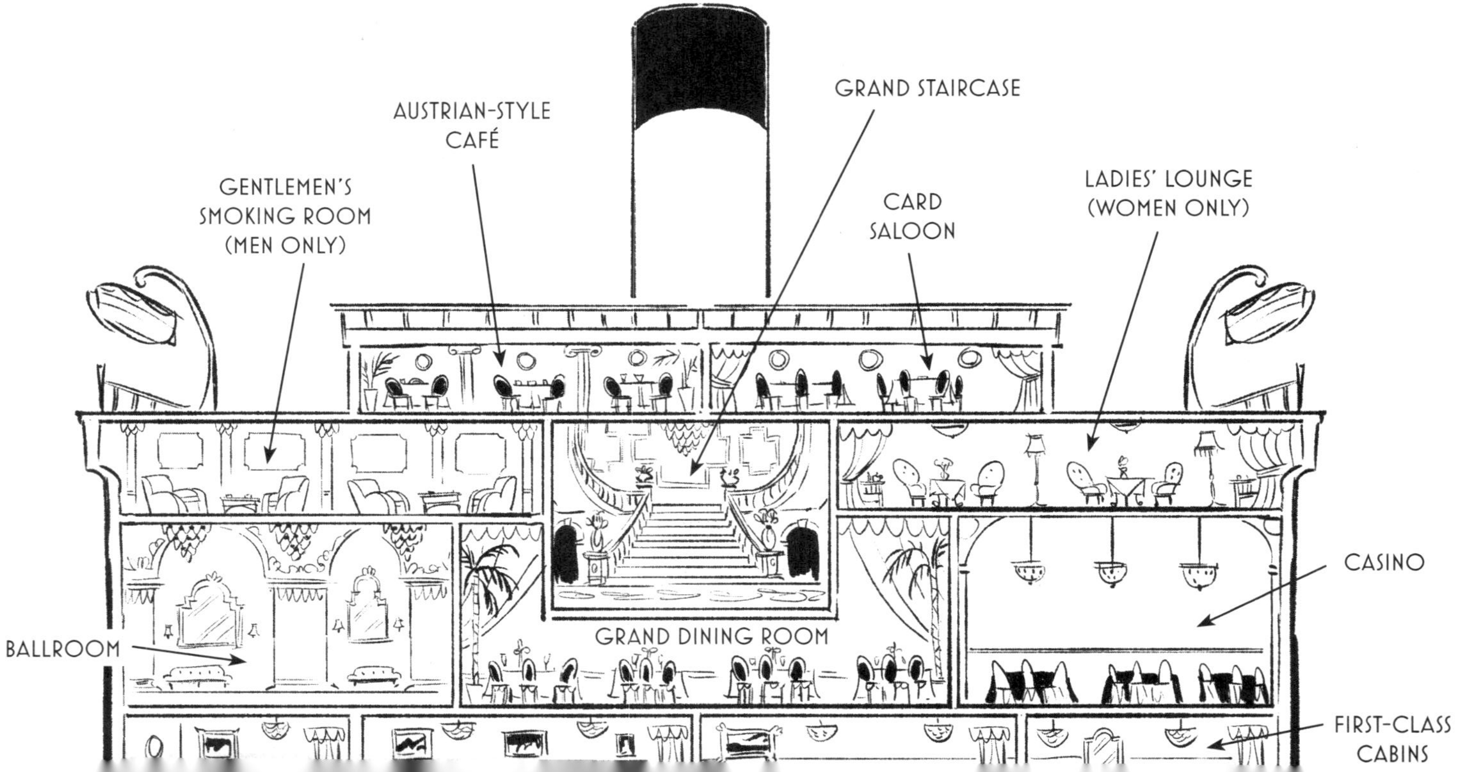

GRAND STAIRCASE

CARD SALOON

AUSTRIAN-STYLE CAFÉ

GENTLEMEN'S SMOKING ROOM (MEN ONLY)

LADIES' LOUNGE (WOMEN ONLY)

CASINO

FIRST-CLASS CABINS

GRAND DINING ROOM

BALLROOM

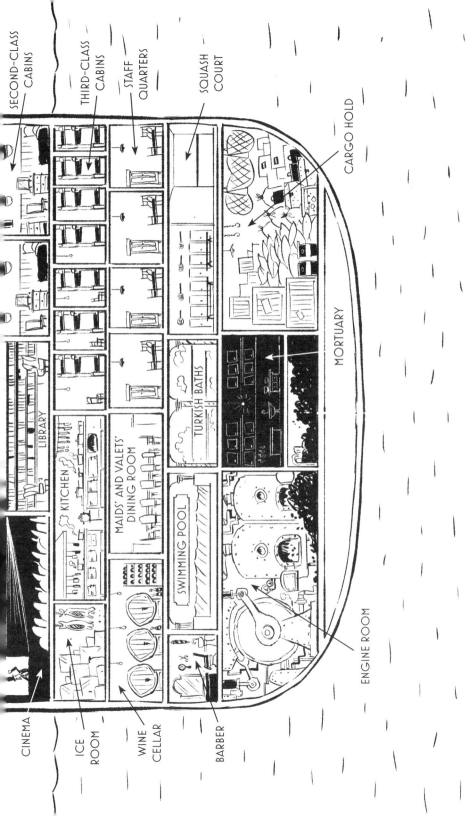

SECOND-CLASS CABINS

THIRD-CLASS CABINS

STAFF QUARTERS

SQUASH COURT

CARGO HOLD

LIBRARY

KITCHEN

MAIDS' AND VALETS' DINING ROOM

TURKISH BATHS

MORTUARY

CINEMA

ICE ROOM

WINE CELLAR

BARBER

SWIMMING POOL

ENGINE ROOM

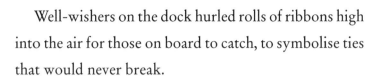

Well-wishers on the dock hurled rolls of ribbons high into the air for those on board to catch, to symbolise ties that would never break.

Others burst into tears, overcome with the heartbreak of saying goodbye.

Many shouted one last "I love you" before the deep hum of the engine drowned them out.

From the deck of the ship, Dilly looked on, wide-eyed with wonder.

This was a musical, a circus, a fireworks display – all rolled into one.

Watson stood on Dilly's shoulders, so as not to be trodden on.

The little dog had a special yelp set aside for that: a high-pitched squeal that Dilly's Auntie Gladys often squeezed out of him, treading on Watson time and time again.

Dilly was returning to England after a whirlwind week in New York.

It was like a dream.

Until a month ago, Dilly had never left the tiny Welsh village where she was born.

It was a poor place. She was from a poor family. Everyone was poor in the village, so Dilly knew nothing else.

Dilly's mam and dad had both died during the Great War.

Dilly was only a baby when they'd died, so she'd never known them. All she had of them were her dad's collection of murder-mystery books, an old black-and-white photograph of him and Mam together, and her mam's smile. In the photo, Dilly's mam looked radiant in her nurse's outfit. Her dad looked striking in his soldier's uniform. They stood arm in arm together, full of pride and life and love. Little did they know that soon tragedy would strike them both down. Just two of the twenty million who died in those four years of war.

It was left to Dilly's Auntie Gladys to care for her. Auntie Gladys might be beautiful on the outside, but she was ugly on the inside. She moved into Dilly's family home, and so began the misery. Gladys hated children, and her niece especially. She called her "the ugly duckling".

Gladys was lazy. She'd never worked a day in her life, so Dilly had to do everything she could to bring in some much-needed money, and sadly there was not much call for paid detective work in their little village. Dilly was up at dawn every morning, mopping the butcher's floor, shovelling coal and sweeping the roads. Then after school she had to work until midnight, scrubbing the school toilets, mucking out pigs and even digging graves. Dilly had to do anything and everything so that she would have something to eat, and her aunt could spend all evening in the pub being bought drinks.

However, overnight everything had changed.

Gladys inherited thousands and thousands of pounds when a distant uncle died. Dilly had never even heard of Great-Uncle Huw, but he must have been rich – richer than rich, because now Dilly and her aunt were suddenly travelling in first-class cabins on a first-class ship. What's more, they had been staying at the swankiest hotel in New York, dining at the finest restaurants and seeing the hottest shows on Broadway. All with Gladys's fancy man, Lord Fox. Fox was the one who had insisted Dilly come along to everything – well, everything except his late-night trips to the casinos! Otherwise, Gladys would have gladly left her behind. Something she always did.

Despite Fox offering to buy the girl lots of expensive presents, Dilly had always said no. She never wanted expensive things.

All she wanted was to be loved.

Instead, Dilly had spent all week in New York watching her aunt shop, shop, shop at the most eye-wateringly, mouth-openingly, bum-clenchingly expensive department stores.

EXHIBIT:

AUNTIE GLADYS

DIAMOND NECKLACE

MATCHING DIAMOND EARRINGS

SILK GLOVES

SILVER WATCH

GOLD BRACELET

FOX-FUR STOLE (WHICH WATSON OFTEN GROWLED AT)

CLOUD OF PERFUME

SILK DRESS

HANDBAG

HIGH-HEELED SHOES

Now that Gladys was rich, she had found what she had always wanted: a fancy man.

And he was *fancy*.

Super fancy.

A dashing English aristocrat named Lord Fox.

The men in the village were never good enough for Gladys. Or, rather, rich enough. She had resisted all their attempts to woo her. She was the prettiest woman in the village, so always attracted attention – all the local women could see through her, but the men were too dazzled by her beauty to think straight.

Auntie Gladys had met Lord Fox at a ball in London for filthy-rich people. It was the kind of thing she went to, now she was filthy rich herself.

Theirs had been a whirlwind romance. Even though they had only known each other for a few weeks, there was already talk of marriage.

At first, Dilly had been suspicious of Fox. Auntie Gladys was drowning in money. Was he pursuing her just so he could get his hands on it?

CHAPTER TWO

OODLES, NOODLES AND POODLES

N_{O.}

Lord Fox, you see, had oodles and noodles and poodles of his *own* money. At a guess, a hundred times what Gladys had inherited.

Dilly didn't care about the money, though. She adored Fox simply because he made her feel special. He would tell her stories, putting on an array of voices for all the characters. He would give her books to read. He liked murder-mystery novels too. In New York, he had even introduced her to the wonderful world of milkshakes.

Banana was her favourite.

Fox made her feel the complete opposite of how her aunt made her feel.

Happy.

EXHIBIT: **LORD FOX**

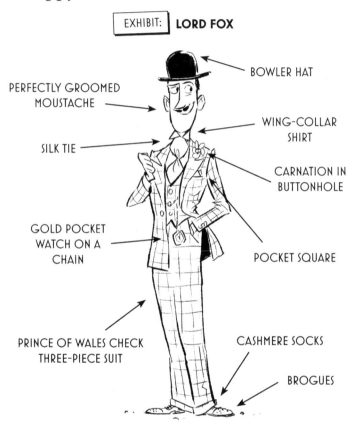

BOWLER HAT

PERFECTLY GROOMED
MOUSTACHE

WING-COLLAR
SHIRT

SILK TIE

CARNATION IN
BUTTONHOLE

GOLD POCKET
WATCH ON A
CHAIN

POCKET SQUARE

PRINCE OF WALES CHECK
THREE-PIECE SUIT

CASHMERE SOCKS

BROGUES

Lord Fox could trace his ancestry back to medieval royalty and would joke about being 112th in line to the throne.

"I only need one hundred and eleven posh people to die, and I will be crowned king!"

Fox lived in a grand stately home named Fox Manor, set in the English countryside.

It had been in the family for hundreds of years. Fox Manor looked stunning from all the photographs he had shown them.

FOX MANOR EXTERIOR

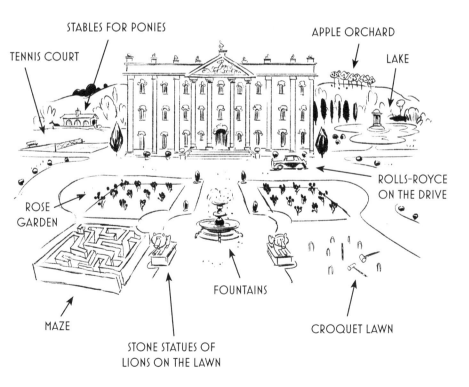

STABLES FOR PONIES

APPLE ORCHARD

TENNIS COURT

LAKE

ROLLS-ROYCE ON THE DRIVE

ROSE GARDEN

MAZE

FOUNTAINS

CROQUET LAWN

STONE STATUES OF LIONS ON THE LAWN

FOX MANOR INTERIOR

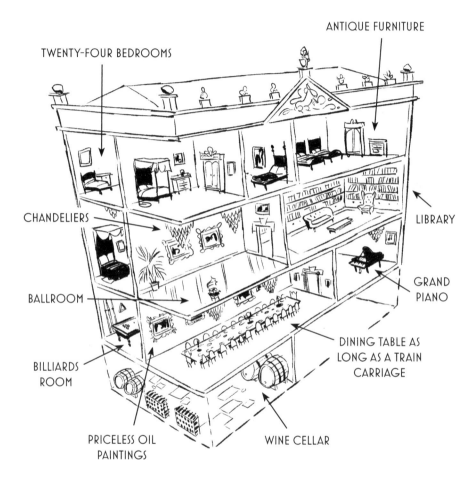

ANTIQUE FURNITURE

TWENTY-FOUR BEDROOMS

CHANDELIERS

LIBRARY

BALLROOM

GRAND PIANO

BILLIARDS ROOM

DINING TABLE AS LONG AS A TRAIN CARRIAGE

PRICELESS OIL PAINTINGS

WINE CELLAR

Whenever Fox showed them a photograph of Fox Manor, Gladys's eyes lit up with glee.

"I would make the perfect Lady Fox!" she would hint, before swishing up and down the room as if she were already lady of the manor. "I always knew I was destined for better things."

"We'd have to be married first, or Mother would not approve!" he would reply.

"A room for my dresses! A room for my shoes! A room for my handbags! And oil paintings of me adorning the walls!"

"And, of course, a room for Dilly and Watson."

Gladys would smile at Lord Fox then. But, as soon as his back was turned, she would hiss to her niece, "The cellar!"

Dilly reasoned that as long as she had her dog and her murder-mystery books, she would get by, although the cellar would get deathly cold in the depths of winter. She would rather not be found frozen solid.

Little did Dilly know that this was precisely the fate that awaited her on board THE MASQUERADE...

CHAPTER THREE

STOP THIS SHIP!

Even though her aunt's elbow was poking her in the eye, with her other eye Dilly took in the spectacular scene of New York at night.

"It's like we're at the centre of the universe!"

"We are," said Fox, smiling. "Never forget how special you are."

"Me?"

"Yes! You! You deserve the world!"

"That's the nicest thing anyone has ever said to me," said Dilly quietly.

Auntie Gladys leaped in. "Apart from all the nice things I say to you on a daily basis, Dilly!"

Dilly smiled thinly. Her aunt had never said a nice thing to her in her life. Well, unless it was in front of Fox. Then she was all sweetness and light. She put on a special mask just for him.

Fox was squashed next to Gladys, among the thousand-strong throng of passengers bustling for the best view of New York.

"You will both become accustomed to all this in time. If you think New York is dazzling, just wait until I take you both on a cruise to Venice."

"Wow! I would love that!" exclaimed Dilly.

Gladys grimaced, before smiling back at Fox.

"To see the most beautiful city in the world reveal itself as the dawn rises is heaven," he said.

"Where is this Venice?" asked Gladys. "Is it somewhere abroad?"

"Italy," replied Dilly.

"She's a right Clever Clogs, this one!" Gladys said.

"Always got her head in some silly book!"

"Murder-mystery books, actually. My father loved them too."

"I would love to know more about him," said Fox. "He sounds like a very special man. A hero."

"He was. And so was my mam."

"Yes! Yes! Yes!" said Gladys. "But sadly they are dead now. I am the real hero! Saved this little one from the orphanage!" she added, patting Dilly on the head awkwardly.

"What a noble thing to do, Gladys," said Fox.

"I know! The perfect woman! Now gimme a kiss!"

With that, Gladys grabbed Fox by the back of his neck and pulled him close for a big sloppy kiss.

"MWAH!"

Yuck, thought Dilly.

She wondered what Fox saw in Gladys beyond her beauty. Dilly constantly had to stop herself from warning him of what a horror her aunt could be. But, if she did, Fox would be gone forever, and she would be left all alone with Gladys again. So she kept silent. For now.

As the horn sounded for THE MASQUERADE to depart…

TOOT!

...Dilly spotted a large figure barging through the crowds on the dock.

"OUT OF THE WAY!" he boomed in an Italian accent. He was wearing a ruffled silk shirt, a velvet bow tie, a velvet blazer and a velvet cape with a shock of red silk lining inside. A shiny top hat completed his striking silhouette. He carried a cane, which he swished to and fro, as if others were mere flies to be swatted.

SWISH! SWUSH! SWOSH!

A platoon of porters trailed after him, carting towers of leather trunks, suitcases and hat boxes.

Dilly recognised him at once!

"THE MAESTRO!" she shouted. "STOP THIS SHIP!"

To a budding detective like Dilly, the Maestro was a legend.

By night, he was a superstar opera singer. By day, he was a master detective. So prodigious were his talents that he had named himself THE MAESTRO!

The Italian word for MASTER!

Being both the greatest tenor of all time **and** the greatest detective of all time made it impossible for him to be humble.

Dilly loved reading about the Maestro's cases. He always made the front page of every newspaper around the world with his powers of deduction, his photographic memory and his peculiar eccentricities.

The Maestro used boot polish to dye his grey hair black. On a hot day, sweaty black goo ran down his face. He ate blancmange for breakfast, lunch and dinner and the many other meals he had invented in between. He scoffed so much of the creamy, sugary, jelly-like dessert that he looked like one.

And he thundered opera arias in the ears of suspects to extract confessions.

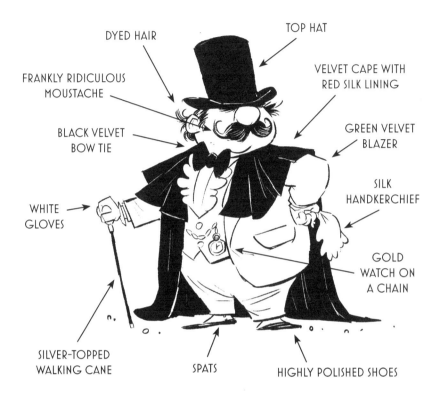

EXHIBIT: **THE MAESTRO**

DYED HAIR

TOP HAT

FRANKLY RIDICULOUS
MOUSTACHE

VELVET CAPE WITH
RED SILK LINING

BLACK VELVET
BOW TIE

GREEN VELVET
BLAZER

SILK
HANDKERCHIEF

WHITE
GLOVES

GOLD
WATCH ON
A CHAIN

SILVER-TOPPED
WALKING CANE

SPATS

HIGHLY POLISHED SHOES

The Maestro's murder cases were famous the world over, all published in his bestselling detective diaries:

- **Floater In The Fountain**
- **Murder By Meatball**
- **The Leaning Tower That Actually Leaned All The Way Over And Fell On Top Of Someone**

- **Silent But Deadly**

- **Evil Under The Salami**

- **The Mamma Mia Murders**

- **The Gelati Assassin**

- **Pope On A Rope**

- **The Concrete Gondola**

- **The Curious Case Of The Pizza Poisoned With Pineapple**

There weren't many people for whom a ship this big would stop, but the Maestro was one of them. THE MASQUERADE juddered to a halt, and the gangplank was secured back into place. Not being a natural athlete, the Maestro struggled to step up on to it, so a couple of porters had to push his ample bottom. Dilly had never seen anyone with so much luggage.

He had even more than Fox.

But, as Fox had explained, a lord needs a special outfit for every occasion.

"CAPTAIN!" boomed the Maestro as he reached the end of the gangway. "WHERE IS THE CAPTAIN?"

The sturdy old captain, who had been busy on the bridge, rushed down to the deck to greet this last-minute passenger. The captain had a white beard and raw skin that had been beaten by rain, wind and snow.

He looked exactly as you would expect a captain to look.

Captainy.

He would be the perfect choice to advertise fish fingers.

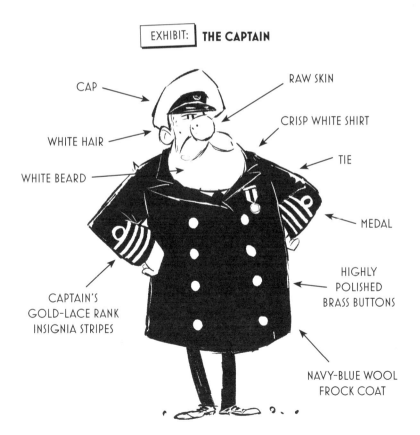

EXHIBIT: **THE CAPTAIN**

CAP

RAW SKIN

CRISP WHITE SHIRT

WHITE HAIR

TIE

WHITE BEARD

MEDAL

CAPTAIN'S GOLD-LACE RANK INSIGNIA STRIPES

HIGHLY POLISHED BRASS BUTTONS

NAVY-BLUE WOOL FROCK COAT

"MAESTRO!" exclaimed the captain over the noise of the engine. "Good evening! What an extraordinary surprise! We weren't expecting you on board!"

"The Maestro has been summoned by the king to sing at the Royal Opera House in London!"

"Oh! We didn't know! Apologies, Maestro. Do you have a ticket?"

"The Maestro doesn't need a ticket! He demands your finest cabin! This instant!"

"I am sorry, Maestro, but our finest cabin is occupied."

"Hurl them over the side! The Maestro gets what the Maestro wants!"

He pushed past the captain and boarded the ship.

Dilly could feel her heart pounding.

Wherever the Maestro went, there was MURDER...

CHAPTER FOUR

POOP DECK

The next morning, Dilly took Watson for a walk along the poop deck. It was just as well, as poop was what Watson needed to do. Well, he couldn't expect to hold it in for the entire week-long voyage. The poor thing would end up the size of a beach ball.

EXHIBIT: **WATSON**

POOP

NO POOP

New York was now far behind them, and **THE MASQUERADE** was powering across the three thousand miles of Atlantic Ocean between America and England. They would not see land for days.

Stampeding straight towards Dilly and Watson was a horde of people, swirling like a school of fish. None of them were looking where they were going. Dilly had to scoop Watson up and leap out of their way to avoid being trampled underfoot.

It was only when the swarm passed that Dilly saw who was creating all this excitement.

THE MAESTRO!

His cape was flapping in the wind, and he was holding on to his hat for fear it would fly off.

Adoring fans were firing questions at him.

"Please, Mr Maestro! May I have your autograph?"

"The Maestro never signs autographs!"

"Please may I take your photograph, sir?"

"When the Maestro has his photograph taken, he has lights, he has make-up, he has hairdressers! That is because the Maestro is a professional! Not an amateur!"

"With a master detective on board, does that mean

there is going to be a murder?"

said one wag, causing much amusement.

"HA! HA! HA!"

The Maestro stopped, and the crowd stopped too. The detective stared at the man. "If you ask one more ridiculous question like that, then it will be you who will be murdered!"

There was an awkward silence for a moment, before the crowd decided it must be a joke, and burst into laughter.

"HA! HA! HA!"

Then the Maestro swished them out of the way with his cane.

SWISH! SWUSH! SWOSH!

Dilly just had to tell the Maestro that she dreamed of being a detective just like him.

"M-M-Maestro…!" she began.

He turned round and gave the girl a disdainful look.

"I am sorry to disturb you—"

But before she could disturb him, the captain interrupted. He was hurrying down the spiral staircase from the bridge, calling out to this VIP: *very important passenger.*

"Ah! Maestro! Good morning, sir! I trust you had a restful night."

"The Maestro had the worst night's sleep of his life!"

"Oh. I am sorry to hear that."

"The bed is too hard. The sheets are as rough as sandpaper! And the boat would not stop rocking!"

"That will be the waves, sir."

"Can't you do anything to stop them?"

"Sadly not, sir."

"But you are the captain!"

"Yes, I am. And I would be honoured if you were to sit at the captain's table tonight for THE MASQUERADE's welcome gala dinner?"

"Will there be blancmange?"

"I shall ask Chef."

"That man is a buffoon! Couldn't boil an egg!"

"He is the most talented chef on the fleet."

"Then the fleet should be torpedoed!"

Just then, a scrambled-egg-coated chef stormed towards them, brandishing a large whisk.

"How dare you hurl scrambled egg over me!" he cried, lunging at the Maestro with his whisk.

The Maestro hid behind Dilly. "Your crumpets were revolting, which is why I only ate nine!"

"How dare you insult my crumpets!"

Chef made another lunge, and the Maestro raised his cane.

A sword fight – well, a cane/whisk fight – commenced.

"NOW STOP! BOTH OF YOU!" ordered the captain, snatching the whisk out of Chef's hand. "Maestro, lower your cane."

Without a word, the legendary singing detective did what he was told. But, as soon as Chef turned away, the Maestro clonked him on the head with it.

K E R L O N K !

"OUCH!"

A triumphant Maestro broke into a triumphant burst of opera…

"*Dilegua, o notte! Tramontate, stelle! Tramontate, stelle! All'alba vincerò! Vincerò! VinceròooooooooooooooooOooooooooooo OOOooooooooooooooooooooOOOO!*"

…and strode off.

He barged past Gladys and Fox.

As he turned into a doorway, the wind whipped up, and his silk handkerchief fell from his breast pocket.

Dilly rushed to pick it up. This wasn't easy, as it was twisting and turning in the wind. When Watson finally caught it, the Maestro was long gone. Dilly coaxed the handkerchief out of her dog's mouth. She admired it for a moment. The richness of the red, the smoothness of the silk, the elegance of the M monogrammed in a corner. It was tempting to keep it, but Dilly's job was to solve crimes, not commit them. Her mam and dad were gone, but she still wanted to make them proud. So she popped the handkerchief into the pocket of her shorts for safekeeping until she next saw the Maestro.

Just then, she had a brilliant idea.

A way she could pick his brains all night!

CHAPTER FIVE
A BIG FAT LIE

"Chef! Back to the kitchen!" ordered the captain.

"I need my whisk!" he pleaded, bursting into floods of tears. "BOO! HOO! HOO!"

He threw his arms round the captain.

"There! There!" said the captain, patting Chef's back. "BOO! HOO! HOO!"

"Come on now. Be a brave chef!"

"BOO! HOO! HOO!"

After an uncomfortably long *boohoohoo*ing, the captain untangled himself from Chef. Then he gave the man his handkerchief.

"Here you go."

But, instead of wiping his eyes, Chef had a good blow.

"HOOOO!"

It was louder than the ship's horn.

He then passed the snotty handkerchief back to the captain, who grimaced before putting it in his pocket.

As the captain sent Chef off, Dilly sidled over to him.

"Good morning, Captain. Can I ask you something?"

"Of course. I get so many questions from children! 'How can I become a captain?' 'Please will you let me steer the ship?' 'Can I try on your cap?' Et cetera."

"No. Nothing like that."

"Oh!"

"I don't want to be a captain. I want to be a detective. It's always been my dream. So please, please, please could I sit at your table for dinner tonight? I really, really, really want to meet the Maestro properly. I need to learn from the master!"

This tickled the captain. "Ha! You are quite the character, Miss…?"

"Dilly. Short for Dilys."

"Miss Dilys, whilst I'm sure you would be marvellous company, sitting at the captain's table on a cruise liner like THE MASQUERADE is an honour granted by my

invitation only. I have hosted kings, queens, presidents, prime ministers and film stars. The table is full tonight. Apologies."

"Oh," she replied, crestfallen.

"Perhaps another night, Miss Dilys. Now please excuse me."

With that, he ascended the staircase with the gusto of a man half his age.

"There must be a way, Watson," she said. "There is always a way."

"RUFF!" agreed her furry assistant.

Gladys and Fox caught up with Dilly.

"What were you talking to the captain about?" Dilly's aunt asked. "I do hope you weren't bothering him!"

"Oh! No, no, no. He was just inviting me, well, us, to sit at his table for dinner."

"Do we *have* to sit with the staff?" asked Gladys.

Fox smiled. "My dear, it is an honour to be invited to sit at the captain's table."

"Is it?"

"Drum roll, please!" said Dilly with a grin. "Guess who else is sitting at the captain's table?"

"The captain?" guessed Gladys.

"Well. Yes. The captain. It's called the captain's table. But also…"

"Not the Maestro?" said Fox.

"YES! It's the chance of a lifetime for a budding detective like me."

"Ho! Ho!" laughed Gladys. "Budding detective! Don't tell the Maestro what you really do! Scrub toilets! Now, what time is dinner?"

"Eight o'clock," replied Fox.

Gladys looked at her new silver watch. "Foxy! That's only ten hours away!" she shrieked. "I'd better start getting ready!"

As she rushed back to her suite, Fox turned to Dilly.

"The captain's table indeed! Clever girl!"

"I try," she replied.

But, as Dilly led Watson away, she wasn't feeling very clever.

She had told a BIG FAT LIE and put herself in DEEP, DEEP DOO-DOO!

CHAPTER SIX

A DANGEROUS MISSION

Dilly had to do something about her lie.

And she could only think of one way.

Make it come true.

In other words, undertake a mission to place herself, Gladys and Fox at the captain's table for dinner.

She and Watson stepped down the grand staircase to the dining room. Peeping through a crack in the double doors, she was greeted by the biggest room she had ever seen in her life. Glittering crystal chandeliers swayed from the ceiling. Full-length antique mirrors adorned the walls. A deep blood-red carpet spread across the floor. There were even live palm trees in enormous pots along the walls.

Before this trip, Dilly had had no clue that rooms like this even existed.

This dining room was already set up for dinner.

The cutlery, glassware and napkins had been arranged perfectly, like this…

EXHIBIT: | **PERFECT PLACE SETTING**

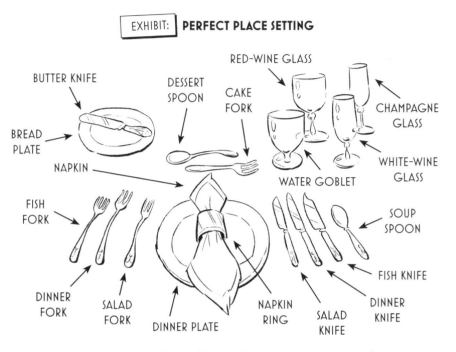

Just as at a posh wedding, there were name cards on each place setting.

Dilly's mission was to swap them around so she could sit right next to the Maestro. It was quite a task finding her name card, as there were so many tables. Eventually, she found it, along with Gladys's and Fox's, on the table furthest from the captain's.

Just as she had snatched the cards and was about

to make her way to the captain's table, DISASTER STRUCK!

The fearsome French maître d' swept into the dining room.

Dilly leaped down out of sight. She got on to all fours, something Watson didn't need to do, and together they hid under a table.

EXHIBIT:

THE MAÎTRE D'

THICK-RIMMED SPECTACLES

DISDAINFUL EXPRESSION

BOW TIE

WHITE GLOVES

DRESS SHIRT WITH SPREAD COLLAR

WHITE SHAWL-COLLARED DINNER JACKET

BLACK TROUSERS WITH SATIN STRIPE

SHOES SO POLISHED HE COULD SEE HIS OWN REFLECTION IN THEM

The maître d' weaved his way around the room, inspecting every place setting. With his white-gloved hands, he meticulously moved cutlery an eighth of an inch until the place settings were perfect.

From under the table, Dilly spied his shoes shuffling from setting to setting until he reached the one on the table above her.

Dilly put her fingers to her lips so Watson wouldn't bark a thing. In turn, Watson put his toe to his lips so she wouldn't say a thing either. For a dog, he was super smart.

The maître d's feet stopped…

This mission was becoming more dangerous by the second.

"What is this?" His French accent was so French he sounded like a comedy Frenchman.

"*Trois* cards missing!"

He began to crouch down to search for the cards under the table.

OUR HEROES WERE ABOUT TO BE BUSTED.

Dilly needed Watson to create a diversion, and fast! She gestured for him to dash from under the table. The dog gestured back with his paw for her to do it instead. Dilly shook her head. Watson sighed, and raced through the maître d's legs.

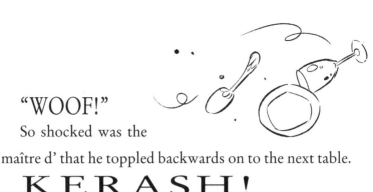

"WOOF!"

So shocked was the

maître d' that he toppled backwards on to the next table.

KERASH!

Cutlery and glassware were sent flying up to the ceiling.

WHOOSH!

Being the meticulous sort, he managed to

grab hold of all the pieces in mid-air. Like an

expert juggler he caught:

a champagne glass in one hand...

three soup spoons and seven

cake forks in the other...

a candelabra on one foot...

an ice bucket on the other...

a butter dish on his head...

a butter knife between

his teeth...

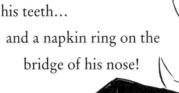

and a napkin ring on the

bridge of his nose!

"*UN CHIEN!* A FILTHY *CHIEN* IN MY DINING ROOM! BEGONE!"

Watson was brave. Instead of rushing straight out, he raced round and round the dining room, barking as loudly as he could.

"WOOF! WOOF! WOOF!"

The man hopped off after him, trying his best not to drop anything.

"I WILL HAVE YOU *GRIL* ALIVE!"

The maître d' was HOPPING MAD!

This mayhem was the diversion Dilly needed.

Still on her hands and knees, she scrambled under the tables until she reached the captain's. She found the Maestro's place card and snatched the three cards to the left of his.

Then she put her card next to his, then Gladys's and then Fox's next to her.

She raced back under the tables, and placed the three original name cards from the captain's table on what had been her table.

BINGO!

Now all she needed to do was get out of the dining room alive.

As the maître d' continued to chase Watson, Dilly began miaowing like a cat.

"MIAOW! MIAOW! MIAOW!"

"*UN CHAT!* A NASTY *CHAT* IN MY DINING ROOM TOO! I WILL HAVE YOU *BOUILLI* ALIVE!"

But, before he could, Dilly had scuttled out of the double doors with Watson close behind.

The doors swung back into the maître d'.

THWUCK!

He was knocked on to another table, this time expertly catching:

a vase of flowers…

a water jug…

a bread basket…

three tumblers…

and a teaspoon, which he balanced on his chin.

The weight of the teaspoon made the maître d' topple

over, landing under a mountain of tableware.

KERASH! KURLANG!
KARUNK!

"NON!" he cried as Dilly and Watson chuckled outside.

"HA! HA!"

CHAPTER SEVEN

A SEA OF GLITZ

Dinner was a sea of glitz.

All the first-class passengers were bedecked in dinner suits and ballgowns.

Tiaras. Silk gloves. Gowns trailing across the floor.

A jazz band made everyone feel as if they were in a musical. They wanted to DANCE! DANCE! DANCE! And after dinner there would be dancing until dawn!

But Dilly barely noticed the ritzy surroundings. She couldn't contain her excitement at the thought of spending the evening picking the brain of the Maestro. She had arrived super early. She was sitting at the captain's table and couldn't help bouncing up and down. To her left was the empty chair where, at any moment now, the Maestro was going to plonk his bottom. Dilly had installed Watson under the table so she could secretly feed him titbits. He had already scoffed three bread rolls and was still pawing for more.

"RUFF!"

Next to arrive were Gladys and Fox. Gladys was wearing a silver ballgown she had bought herself in New York. It must have cost a bomb, but she looked like a turkey wrapped in tinfoil.

Fox was wearing white tie and tails. The shirt collar was a little worn, the leather shoes were cracked and there was even a tiny moth-hole in the jacket. It was the aristocratic way of dressing. These clothes and shoes were hand-made to last a lifetime. In posh circles it was considered vulgar to wear things that were brand new.

His manners were impeccable. He pulled out Gladys's chair for her to sit.

Then he took her gloved hand and kissed it, before gently stroking her cheek.

"Gladys, you couldn't look more beautiful tonight."

"I know," she replied, shooting a look at Dilly like the cat that got the cream.

Soon, other guests joined the table.

A rich American lady, who had dragged her mortified daughter along so she could find her a suitor.

A suave Swiss tennis champion.

A Hungarian scientist, known only as the Professor, who was working on a top-secret project to build a mega bomb. However, he kept boasting about it to everyone, so it wasn't top secret any more.

A cardinal, second-in-command to the Pope.

A famous jazz trumpet player and singer, known as Satchmo.

The maître d' swept over to the table, sporting a black eye, no doubt from being clonked by a soup spoon.

He eyeballed the three interlopers.

These weren't the guests he had placed on the captain's table!

"These aren't your seats! You must move at once!"

"But the captain placed us here himself," lied Dilly.

"You are not VIPs!"

"No. We are VVIPs! Very, VERY important people. This is my Auntie Gladys, and this is her special friend, LORD Fox."

"Good evening," purred the lord.

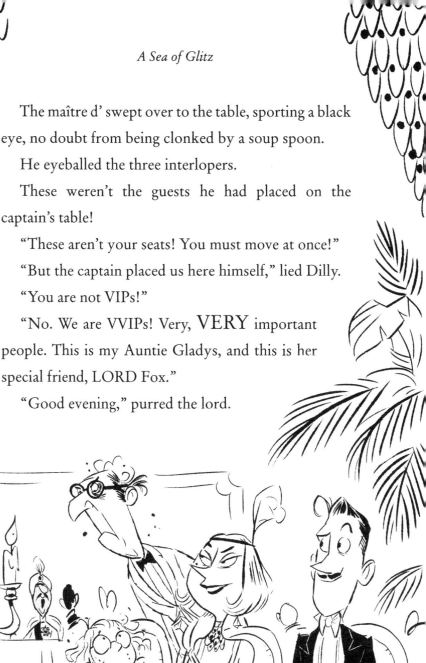

Fear flashed in the maître d's eyes. It was incredible to see his reaction to that word: "lord". Suddenly the maître d' was bent double, grovelling.

"YOUR HIGHNESS!" he said, his voice sounding like oil. "Please, please, please forgive me!"

"You are forgiven," replied Fox with a wry smile.

"*Merci! Merci! Merci!* I do so want to keep my job," the maître d' said.

Then he called across the dining room to the nearest waiter. "CHAMPAGNE! A BOTTLE OF OUR FINEST CHAMPAGNE FOR OUR ROYAL LORDSHIP!"

"Oooh! Thank you!" said Gladys.

"And a banana milkshake, please," added Dilly.

"BANANA MILKSHAKE! A GLASS OF OUR FINEST BANANA MILKSHAKE FOR *MADEMOISELLE!*"

"Thank you," she replied, not that the maître d' would have heard, as he was already racing to the kitchen.

"Gladys, dearest," said Fox.

"What?"

"I hate to be impolite, but you are only wearing one earring."

"I am sure I put it on!"

She reached up to her ears.

"NO!" she exclaimed.

"There is no need to…"

"No need to what? I look like a clown sitting here with one earring! And these are the diamond ones you got me in New York! I gotta get back to my cabin and find it!"

"Please, allow me."

"But…"

"Please. Just give me your key and I will find it for you."

"It must still be in my jewellery box."

"See you in moments, my sweet."

Glady handed him her cabin key. He smiled, bowed and hurried off.

"My Foxy's a proper gent, ain't he?"

"He certainly is," agreed Dilly.

"Nothing like the riffraff from round our way!"

"I like riffraff."

"Of course you do! You are the riffiest raffiest riffraff there is!" she hissed. "But I always knew I was special! Better than everyone else in the village. That must be why he's fallen head over heels in love with me!"

"I am happy you are happy."

"That's strange, because I'm only happy when you are unhappy."

"No surprise there," muttered Dilly.

"Ooh! It's all been so fast. I bet before we reach England my Foxy will propose!"

"But you've only known him for a few weeks."

"Love is love! And I'll get a great big juicy diamond ring! I spied him disappearing off to the swankiest jeweller's in New York! But do you know what the best part is?"

"No."

"If all goes to plan, I will move straight into Fox Manor!"

"I will need to go and collect my dad's books from home."

"Oh! We're never going back to that dump!"

"Never?"

"No!"

"Why?"

"I sold it!"

Dilly couldn't believe what she was hearing. "You sold it?"

"Yep!"

"But it's not yours to sell! It was my mam and dad's home! And I wanted to live there when I'm older!"

"Mam and Dad are dead! I am the boss of you! I could have dumped you in an orphanage! And I still can! Remember that, you ungrateful wretch!"

"What about my books?"

"Tossed on a bonfire!"

"BUT…"

But before Dilly could say another word the captain arrived at the table looking immaculate in his dress uniform, his medals clinking as he moved.

"Good evening!" he said, before spotting the cheeky scamp. "What are you doing sitting here, Miss Dilys?"

"Oh! The maître d' moved us."

"I thought you said it was the captain!" said Gladys.

At that moment the maître d' appeared with a magnum of vintage champagne.

"The finest champagne for his lordship," he announced.

"Lordship?" asked the captain.

"Yes!" replied Gladys. "My fiancé! Well, soon to be fiancé! He just dashed back to my cabin to fetch my earring!"

"Pardon me, madam! Of course, you are most welcome on my table. Now where is our guest of honour, the Maestro?"

The captain looked around the dining room, but the Maestro was nowhere to be seen.

Soon after, a door swung open.

THWUCK!

A one-armed man dressed in a red military jacket stumbled in. He was roaring drunk and staggered about, swigging from a bottle of brandy.

He thumped into a table, knocking over the glassware, much to the diners' horror.

"GASP!"

"STEADY ON!"

The maître d' scurried over, took the man by his arm and tried to lead him out. "Please, *monsieur*, you are making an exhibition of yourself!"

"UNHAND ME, MAN! I AM A BRIGADIER!"

"You are drunk, Brigadier!"

"I'VE BARELY HAD A BOTTLE! NOW

UNHAND ME OR I WILL BE FORCED TO CALL IN THE INFANTRY!"

"Please, Brigadier, let me escort you back to your *cabine*!" he said.

The brigadier was having none of it.

"CHARGE!"

He took a swing at the maître d', but was so sozzled he punched himself in the face.

He spun round, crashing through the double doors into the kitchen. The captain leaped to his feet…

"Excuse me!"

…and hurried after him.

"Well, I didn't know they put on a show too!" cooed Auntie Gladys.

The maître d' intercepted the captain. "*Capitaine,* should I wait to serve *le diner* until *le* Maestro is here?"

The captain inspected his watch. "No, no, no, we are already running late," he replied. "After that scene with the brigadier, we need to steer our passengers out of choppy waters. Instruct the waiters to bring out the first course."

"Very good, *Capitaine.*"

"I am sure the Maestro will join us soon."

But he never did.

CHAPTER EIGHT
THE FIRST MURDER

"One diamond earring. And one key," announced Fox as he returned to the table.

"Oh! You're wonderful!" cooed Gladys.

"Allow me," he said, gently clipping the earring to her ear. "You look more beautiful than ever."

"I know!" she replied.

"You missed some drama," said Dilly.

"Drama? What drama?" he asked.

"A bonkers brigadier!" exclaimed Gladys. "He was a hoot! Drunk as a skunk! Oi, Captain! You should get him to sit here! He would liven things up! This lot are right boring!"

The other diners looked at her, offended.

Fox seemed eager to change tack.

"A huge pleasure to meet you, Captain," he said.

"No, Lord Fox. It's an honour to have you at my table."

"But where is the Maestro? I am eager to meet the great man. As is the delightful Dilly here!"

Dilly glowed red.

"Yes, I know," said the captain, offering a wry smile.

Gladys was jealous when her niece received the slightest attention, and so immediately changed the subject.

"Now where is this opera bloke? I want dessert!"

"I have dispatched my second-in-command, the first officer, to the Maestro's cabin. The Maestro won't want to miss the blancmange. Chef has created an especially large one for him that will feed not just the Maestro but the entire ship!"

"YUM!" said Dilly.

Moments later, the first officer approached the table and whispered in the captain's ear. Dilly watched them like a hawk. Being a detective, she had to. She couldn't hear what was being said, but she didn't need to. From the captain's expression, she could tell something was wrong.

The Maestro could not be found.

Dilly "accidentally" dropped a spoon.

"OOPS!"

Then she slid under the table.

"Watson!" she whispered.

The dog had now eaten so many titbits that he was lying on his back with his legs in the air, in a FOOD COMA.

Dilly nudged her dog, and he woke up with a bark.

"WOOF!"

"SHUSH!" she shushed. "I need you to find the owner of this."

Dilly whipped the master detective's handkerchief out of her shorts. She pushed it against Watson's nose so he could follow the Maestro's scent. The dog nodded and sneaked out from under the table, his nose to the carpet.

Dilly reappeared holding her spoon. "Here it is!"

"That took you a while," sneered Gladys.

"There were a lot of spoons down there," lied Dilly. "I just needed to find the right one!"

"Excuse me, Captain," said the maître d'. "Should I wheel out the blancmange?"

"Yes. Maestro or no Maestro, it's very late. We need to serve dessert now."

The maître d'
hurried to the
kitchen before

throwing open the double doors dramatically, wheeling out a colossal blancmange.

"MAY I PRESENT TO YOU… THE *BLANC-MANGER!*" he announced.

It is not often a blancmange receives a round of applause, but this one did.

Satchmo even played a fanfare on his trumpet!

"TOOT! TOOOT! TOOOOOT!"

This blancmange was so big you could take a bath in it.

"CAPTAIN!" cried the maître d'. "PLEASE DO US ALL THE HONOUR OF SERVING THE FIRST SPOONFUL!"

The captain rose from his seat to slightly less enthusiastic applause.

The maître d' handed him a spoon the size of a sink.

With a flourish, the captain plunged it into the blancmange.

"TA-DA!"

Something large, Italian and operatic oozed out.

IT WAS THE BODY OF THE MAESTRO.

SPLURGE!

The diners all screamed. "AAARRRGGGHHH!"

Watson charged in!

"WOOF!"

The dog had followed the Maestro's scent! He leaped on top of his body and licked the cream off his face.

"SLURP!"

SUCCESS! WATSON HAD FOUND HIM!

Just a smidge too late.

ACT II

DEATH BY ICE

CHAPTER NINE

BLOOD ON THE WHISK

When the master detective is murdered, who is left to solve the mystery?

Dilly and Watson! That's who!

Later that night, the detective duo sneaked out of their cabin. There was sleuthing to be done.

It was now the early hours of the morning, and they were supposed to be tucked up in bed. The captain had ordered all passengers to barricade themselves in their cabins for the night.

THERE WAS A MURDERER ON THE LOOSE!

Until he or she was caught, everyone had to be on RED ALERT.

To be a sleuth, you had to be fearless. And Dilly was fearless. Well, at least she pretended to be, for Watson's sake. Watson was fearless too. Well, at least he pretended to be, for Dilly's sake.

The pair tiptoed along the gangways and down the stairs until they reached the dining room. The double doors were locked.

IT WAS NOW A CRIME SCENE.

So the pair had to make their way to the kitchen. Fortunately, being on the small side, they could climb into the dumb waiter that took them two floors down.

Dilly's hand crept along the wall like a spider until she found a light switch.

TICK!

The vast kitchen revealed itself.

There must have been PANDEMONIUM!

After the Maestro's dead body had been discovered, the cooks must have abandoned their posts and fled the scene.

"Now where did they make this blancmange?" Dilly asked herself.

On the floor were lines in the grease made by the wheels of the trolley.

"WOOF!" barked Watson, pointing to them with his nose.

"Clever boy!"

The pair followed the lines to a

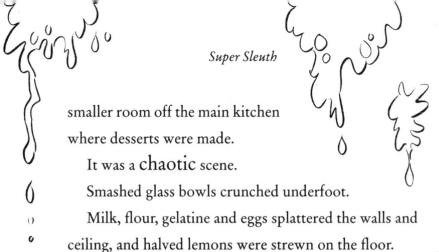

smaller room off the main kitchen
where desserts were made.

It was a chaotic scene.

Smashed glass bowls crunched underfoot.

Milk, flour, gelatine and eggs splattered the walls and
ceiling, and halved lemons were strewn on the floor.

Pots and pans lay upturned everywhere.

Dilly found Chef's battered* hat on the floor.

Using his super-sniff power, Watson found a vital

* BATTERED AS IN BROKEN. NOT AS IN DEEP-FRIED.

clue under the counter. He squeezed himself out from under it, holding the big steel whisk between his teeth.

"Excellent work, Watson!" whispered Dilly as she took it from his mouth.

Tugging her magnifying glass out of her satchel, she examined the whisk closely. It had specks of blood on it.

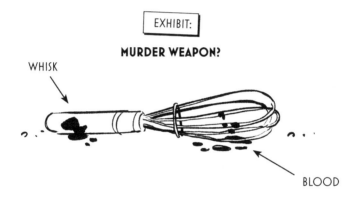

EXHIBIT:

MURDER WEAPON?

WHISK

BLOOD

"Could Chef have used this to knock out the Maestro before he drowned in blancmange?" she asked herself.

Looking down at the floor, Dilly spied footprints in the flour. It looked like one of those diagrams of feet showing you how to do a dance. Dilly took her detective's notebook and sketched the pattern of the footprints. The lead in her pencil snapped, so she had to use her spare pencil. That still left her spare, spare pencil in case of emergency.

For now.

EXHIBIT:

CRIME SCENE

FLOUR

FOOTPRINTS

"The chief suspect must be Chef. He even had a motive! The Maestro insulted his crumpets. And no one likes their crumpets insulted. We need to find Chef, so I can question him."

Dilly put Chef's hat under the dog's nose. "Watson, follow this scent!"

The dog darted off, Dilly trailing behind.

"SNIFF! SNIFF! SNIFF!"

Watson didn't stop sniffing until they had reached the stern of the ship. A thick fog had descended on

THE MASQUERADE. There, on the deck, was a pile of discarded clothes. It was Chef's uniform.

"WOOF!"

"YES! YOU DID IT AGAIN!"

Dilly leaned over the rail.

Immediately, she felt dizzy.

It was a long drop into the ocean.

THE MASQUERADE was moving fast. If Chef had leaped into the waves, he would be long gone.

Just then Dilly felt a figure looming behind her. She froze in TERROR!

CHAPTER TEN

OUT OF THE FOG

"**G**RRRR!" growled Watson from behind Dilly.

As she heard ripping…

RRRIIIIIP!

…she spun round.

There was an unusually short fellow, shorter than her, fighting off her dog with his leg.

"GET THIS BEAST AWAY FROM ME!" he yelled in a Russian accent.

The little man had long black hair parted in the middle, and an even longer black beard. He walked with a stick that was taller than him.

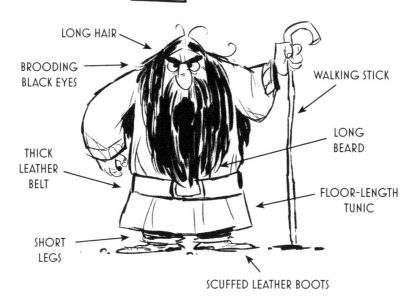

LONG HAIR

BROODING
BLACK EYES

WALKING STICK

LONG
BEARD

THICK
LEATHER
BELT

FLOOR-LENGTH
TUNIC

SHORT
LEGS

SCUFFED LEATHER BOOTS

"WHO ARE YOU?" demanded Dilly.

"MOROSOV!" he replied.

"Who?"

"Russia's greatest novelist! Of all time! Now get this
fiend off me!"

"Watson!"

The dog reluctantly retreated.

"GRRR!"

"Good boy." Dilly turned to the Russian man. "Now
what were you doing creeping up behind me?"

"I had something important to tell you."

"Go on, then."

"I noticed you were doing some detective work."

"Yes, me and Watson are a crime-solving duo."

"RUFF!" agreed Watson.

"Ooh!" she said, remembering he'd said he was a novelist. "Do you write detective books?"

"PAH!" he snapped. "PAH! PAH! And PAH again! I would never lower myself to that indignity. Trash! All of it trash. I write from the depths of my soul. Have you never heard of *From Despair to Nowhere?*"

"Sorry, no."

"*Desolation of the Psyche?*"

"No."

"*The Futility of Existence?*"

"No."

"*Darkness Only Darkness?*"

"No."

"*The Heart of Stone? Love is a Catastrophe? The Depths of Misery?*"

"No, no and no. To be honest, I only read murder-mystery novels. But these all sound super-duper-wuper fun."

Watson shook his head. Clearly, he had no intention of reading them either.

"Now, Morosov, you were about to tell me something…? Something important, you said."

"Yes. I was sitting at dinner tonight… And I witnessed the Maestro ooze out of the blancmange. His death is not a great loss to the classical-music world. Sounded like a foghorn!"

"Is that what you had to tell me?"

"Patience, child. I took a stroll out on the deck after dinner, coming up with ideas for my new book, *The Smell of Fear*, and saw Chef climbing out from behind one of the lifeboats. He must have been hiding."

Now Dilly was intrigued. "Go on…"

"Chef ran to this very spot," he said, tapping his walking stick on the deck. "Then stripped down to his undercrackers…"

"Thank goodness he was wearing some."

"And, before I could stop him, he leaped from the ship, and plunged into the sea."

"Oh no!"

"Oh yes! Chef must have murdered the Maestro, and then tried to escape by swimming back to America."

Dilly did not buy this.

"That would be impossible. It's too far. Too cold. And you would end up as shark food."

"Yes. Chef must be long dead by now. And no trace of him will ever be found."

She eyed the man with suspicion. "How do you know Chef murdered the Maestro?"

Morosov laughed. "Ha! Ha! And I thought you were the detective!"

"I *am* the detective."

"WOOF!"

"I mean WE are the detectives," she added.

Watson nodded.

"Well, isn't it obvious, child?" said Morosov. "The Maestro insulted his crumpets, covered him in scrambled egg, whacked him over the head with his cane, so Chef took his revenge! Drowned him in a giant blancmange."

"It looks that way."

"It is that way."

At that moment, another figure took shape in the fog.

"WHAT ARE YOU DOING OUT HERE?" he barked. It was the captain. "I ORDERED ALL PASSENGERS TO STAY IN THEIR CABINS!"

As he strode towards them, Dilly looked back to where Morosov had been standing…

…BUT HE WAS GONE.

He had disappeared into the fog like a dream.

Just then the captain shouted…

"MISS DILYS!"

Dilly thought of doing a runner, before whispering, "I think he knows it's me, Watson."

The dog hit his head with a paw, knowing it was he who was the brains behind it all.

"WHY ARE YOU OUT OF YOUR CABIN?" demanded the captain as he drew near.

"Oh, good evening, Captain."

"It's morning now. Answer the question."

"We're doing detective work."

"But you are a child. And Watson is a dog!"

"I applaud your powers of observation! Do you want to see my first big clue?"

The question hung in the fog for a moment.

"Go on…"

"Look. Here are Chef's clothes."

The captain peered down to inspect them.

"Yes. They're his all right. He must have jumped overboard."

"It looks that way, but it all seems… too perfect."

"Miss Dilys! This is not a murder-mystery novel. The murderer is dead. And now we can all sleep safely in our beds."

"There was a witness who said he saw Chef jump."

"Who?"

"A Russian novelist. Writes only really, really, really miserable books. Morosov."

"Morosov?"

"You must know him. He told me he is famous."

The captain repeated the name, rolling it round his mouth and his brain.

"Morosov. Morosov. Morosov. I don't recall seeing the name Morosov on my passenger list. What did he look like?"

"Short. Like, really short. Like, up to here," she said, indicating her chest. "Long black hair, long black beard."

"Where is this Morosov now?"

Dilly felt hesitant. She knew her answer would sound far-fetched.

"He disappeared."

"Disappeared?"

Dilly nodded.

The captain looked at her with suspicious eyes. "Are you sure you didn't invent this Morosov character, Miss Dilys?"

"YE-ES!" she replied, her voice cracking as if she were lying.

This only deepened the captain's suspicion. "I will investigate this further, but, for now, back to your cabin!"

"WOOF!" complained Watson.

"BOTH OF YOU! You must lock the door and not leave until the morning."

With that, the captain bundled up Chef's uniform.

"What are you doing?" said Dilly. "This is a crime scene!"

"I don't want to alarm my passengers any further! They have already seen a dead detective ooze out of a blancmange. Not the best way to begin the cruise. Now follow me."

Dilly's eye was caught by something on the deck, which had been hidden under Chef's clothes.

It was an orange stain. Her curiosity got the better of her, and she bent down to inspect it.

"What are you doing now?" demanded the captain.

Dilly dabbed her finger on the stain, before bringing it up to her nose.

"Alcohol!" she said.

"Are you sure?"

She offered her fingertip to the captain to double-check. He sniffed. "Brandy."

"The brigadier was holding a bottle of it. That places him here at the scene too."

"Any passenger could have spilled it."

"Here? Right at the spot where Chef's clothes were found? Don't you think that's a coincidence?"

"Miss Dilys!" said the captain. "I think it is time you two were tucked up in bed. Now come on! I will escort you back to your cabin. Quick march!"

But Dilly was not giving up.

Not until she had solved the murder!

CHAPTER ELEVEN

THE PLOT THICKENS

Dilly couldn't sleep a wink.

Her mind was racing with the drama of the night.

The dead body in the blancmange.

The scene of devastation in the kitchen.

The blood-spotted whisk.

The abandoned chef's uniform.

The mysterious Morosov.

The drop of brandy on the deck.

Dilly took out her notebook and began scribbling down every detail she could remember.

What?

When?

Where?

Who?

Why?

Turning back a page, she looked at the sketch she had

made of the footprints on the kitchen floor. On closer examination, she realised these weren't the prints of two pairs of feet. But *three*.

You could tell not just by the size of the footprints, but also by the direction in which they travelled.

Chef must be one.

Maestro the other.

So, who did this third pair of feet belong to?

And why were they involved in the struggle?

Could it have been the brigadier?

THE PLOT THICKENED.

Dilly sat on the edge of her huge bed. She patted it, and Watson took a running jump. The silk sheet was so smooth that the dog couldn't stop.

WHIZZ!

Instead, he slid off the bed and landed on the rug.

THWOMP!

The rug was silk too. It slid across the highly polished floor, taking Watson with it.

SWOOSH!

"WOOF!"

He collided with a pouffe...

BOFF!

...soared over the sofa...

WHIZZ!

...and landed headfirst in the laundry basket.

"WOOF!" barked Watson, his little furry back legs waggling.

Dilly leaped up, did her best to wipe the smile off her face and pulled Watson out.

When he emerged, his nose had become stuck in a smelly sock.

"WOOF!"

Dilly scooped him into her arms and yanked the sock off his nose.

"WOOF!"

"I know, I know. Poor thing. Come on."

She carried Watson across the cabin and set him down gently on the bed. Then she stroked him. He nuzzled up against her, before rolling on his tummy, completely surrendering to her love.

"If we are to solve our very first murder case," she said, "we need to get some sleep."

Just as well, as her dog was already snoring away. "ZZZZ!"

Later that day, the captain returned to Dilly's cabin.

"Miss Dilys, last night I sent a telegram to Scotland Yard in London, alerting the police to the Maestro's murder. And, of course, Chef's leap from the ship. They agreed it was an open-and-shut case."

Dilly huffed. "The case isn't shut. There are too many things that don't make sense. Did you check your passenger list?"

"Yes. There is no passenger named Morosov on board THE MASQUERADE."

"But I saw him with my own eyes!"

"Please tell me the truth, Miss Dilys. Did you invent him?"

"NO."

"RUFF!" agreed Watson.

"The truth!"

Just as Dilly was about to unravel, Auntie Gladys entered the cabin, all dressed up.

Hair.

Make-up.

New dress.

New handbag.

New shoes.

"Good morning, madam," said the captain.

"Aye, aye, Captain! Thank you for a super supper last night."

"Super?" he asked.

"Well, until the blancmange was wheeled out. The dead body did put me right off my dessert."

Fox appeared too.

"Oh! Good morning, Captain. To what do we owe the pleasure?"

Dilly gave the captain a look that begged...

PLEASE DON'T GRASS ME UP!

This made him smile. "Oh! I was just checking in on all my passengers after the tragic events of last night. You will be relieved to know the murderer leaped into the ocean."

"Who was he, or she?" asked Fox.

"Chef!"

Fox thought for a moment. "Hmm. That makes sense. Chef had a strong motive."

"Hang on a moment!" said Gladys.

All eyes turned to her. Was she about to crack the case?

"Yes…?" prompted Dilly.

"If Chef's dead, then who's cooking me breakfast?"

"Please don't worry," replied the captain with a hint of a smile. "We have a team of the very finest cooks on board."

"Thank goodness for that!"

"If you'd be kind enough to follow me," said the captain, "it would be a pleasure to escort you all to the breakfast room."

After breakfast, during which Dilly sneaked her banger under the table for Watson, the pair slunk off to continue their sleuthing. Walking the dog was always the perfect excuse.

The detective duo returned to the stern of the ship. Passengers were parading up and down as if nothing had happened.

Of course, Chef's clothes had been bundled away, so there was no clue that this was where he may have leaped to his death. As much as she tried, Dilly couldn't find the orange brandy spot on the deck any more. Had it been worn away underfoot? Or had

someone returned during the night and scrubbed it off?

"It's gone, Watson," she said.

The dog put his nose to the floor and, after some serious sniffing, found another spot of brandy, then another and another.

"SNIFF! SNIFF! SNIFF!"

"Watson! You clever boy! Keep following the scent!"

THE MASQUERADE was heading into a storm. Dark clouds swirled overhead. At first the rain was sharp pinpricks of water, before lightning shocked the sky and thunder roared.

CRACK! BOOM!

Then hard rain swept in, battering everyone and everything in sight.

DISASTER!

It washed away the trail of brandy spots from the deck.

"Go, go , go, Watson!" shouted Dilly over the storm's uproar.

"SNIFF! SNIFF! SNIFF!"

The dog did his best, but now there was no scent to follow.

Dilly wasn't going to give up. Wiping the rainwater from her eyes, she spotted three doors. Each one led to a different part of the ship.

As passengers hurried inside, Watson hurtled to the middle door and ran round in circles.

"Watson! How do you know…?"

But, as soon as they were inside, Dilly spotted another brandy spot on the floor. **"WATSON! YOU'RE A GENIUS!"**

The dog's tongue rolled out. He was smiling. Then he shook the rain off his coat, spraying water everywhere, and put his nose back to the floor.

"SNIFF!"

The spots led down a grand staircase into the depths of **THE MASQUERADE**.

They stopped at a huge metal door, which was ice-cold to the touch.

Watson pressed his paw against it. This was the end of the trail.

"GOOD BOY, WATSON!"

He sat neatly, although he slid back on the floor because of his wet bottom.

SQUEAK!

This was a cue for Dilly to give him a treat. She took a dog biscuit out of her satchel, and Watson devoured it in half a second.

"CHOMP!"

A sign on the door read: **DANGER! KEEP OUT!**

Dilly wasn't the kind of girl to let that stop her.

In fact, it was a GREEN LIGHT FOR GO!

Using all her might, she turned the handle and pulled open the thick door.

Instantly, she was hit by a blast of cold air.

WHOOSH!

As the mist cleared, Dilly peered in.

IT WAS THE ICE ROOM.

CHAPTER TWELVE

A FROZEN FOREST

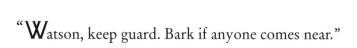

"Watson, keep guard. Bark if anyone comes near."

"WOOF!"

Dilly stepped inside.

The ice room was seriously spooky.

Black as night.

Air so cold it burned the skin.

Dilly took a deep breath.

Her lungs filled with arctic air.

For a moment, she felt as though she was going to freeze solid from the inside out.

Then she timed her breaths with her steps, slow and steady.

The carpet of snow crunched underfoot.

KERUNCH!

Dilly took a candle and a box of matches from her satchel. She needed a few goes to light the match, as she was shaking with fear and cold. Her coat was soaked through from the storm, the rain crystallising into ice.

Eventually, the flame flickered, and the candle illuminated the room.

There were hundreds of blocks of ice, all different shapes and sizes. They had been fished out of the sea by the crew as **THE MASQUERADE** powered through icefields.

A FROZEN FOREST.

"HUH!" she screamed as she bumped into a huge rack of meat that was hanging from the ceiling.

And another.

"HUH!"

And another.

"HUH!"

And another.

"HUH!"

Chickens, geese, ducks. Plucked and headless.

Frozen fish suspended in barrels of ice.

Lobster, crab, octopus. Ready to be cooked and served on silver platters.

There was enough food down here to feed an army.

Dilly didn't know what she was looking for. But she was sure she would know what it was when she found it.

Clues are like that.

It could be a bullet.

It could be a bite out of a biscuit.

It could be just a stray hair.

It didn't matter what it was, just that you had found one.

Part of her wanted to turn back, but a bigger part of her wanted to carry on.

Her brain felt as if it was slowing with the cold.

To prevent it from shutting down completely, Dilly had to keep thinking, thinking, thinking.

Why would the brigadier stumble into the deep-freeze room?

What was he doing here?

And did he ever come out alive?

Just as Dilly thought the ice room must be coming

to an end, more and more of it revealed itself. Was it the entire length of THE MASQUERADE?

Still, Dilly hadn't come this far to give up now.

The flicker of the flame danced off the icebergs, creating kaleidoscopes of light.

Out of the corner of her eye, Dilly saw something that made her stop dead.

This iceberg was different.

There was a shape. An outline. A figure.

Slowly, she pressed her candle up against it and…

"ARGH!"

…found a frozen face staring back at her!

IT WAS CHEF!

Wearing only his undercrackers!

Entombed in a block of ice!

His dead body was so cold it had turned blue!

In shock, Dilly dropped her candle and ran back

towards the misty doorframe. But, as she drew nearer, she saw a silhouette of someone wrestling Watson away.

"WOOF! WOOF! WOOF!"

"STOP!" cried Dilly.

Then the shadowy figure moved, and suddenly the door was being closed on her. The shaft of light in the doorway was becoming slimmer and slimmer.

"NOOOO!" she cried as she hurled herself at the door.

SHUNT!

It slammed shut.

"HELP! HELP! LET ME OUT! I BEG YOU! I WILL DIE IN HERE!"

Dilly thumped on the door.

THUD! THUD! THUD!

The freezing metal stung the palms of her hands. They felt like they were on fire.

CLUNK!

The door was locked.

Dilly's fingers searched her satchel for her paperclip. But by the time she had found it her hands were shaking uncontrollably, and she couldn't pick the lock.

"HHHHHEEEEELLLLLP!"

But, in here, no one could hear her scream.

Still Dilly cried and thumped, thumped and cried,
until she could cry and thump no more.

The air in her lungs iced up.

Her heartbeat slowed to a stop.

Her blood froze solid.

THIS MUST BE THE END...

CHAPTER THIRTEEN

AN ICE-COLD COFFIN

Dilly blacked out.

She toppled backwards on to a block of ice.

KERUNCH!

The force of her fall shattered it.

She lay on the bed of shards.

Soon, they fused to her, encasing her in ice.

AN ICE-COLD COFFIN!

But then, just as her heart slowed to a stop, the door was flung open.

SWING!

"OFF! OFF!"

It was the captain.

"GRRRR!"

And Watson, tugging on his trouser leg.

The dog must have dragged the captain all the way

down here. No wonder his trouser leg had been ripped to shreds.

"GRRR!"

Watson gave one last yank, and the trouser leg swept clean off.

RIP!

Now the captain was showing a lot of leg. A whole leg, in fact. A hairy leg.

It was the strangest pair of trousers.

EXHIBIT:

TROUSER SHORTS

ONE-LEG TROUSERS

ONE-LEG
SHORTS

These trouser shorts might wow on a Paris catwalk, but they looked super silly on the captain.

"HOLD STILL, MISS DILYS!" he ordered, even though it was impossible for her to move.

He slipped off his boot and whacked the ice.

THUMP!

The ice splintered.

CRACK!

Watson leaped on to his mistress, licking her face furiously.

"SLURP! SLURP! SLURP!"

One eye opened. Then the other.

Dilly gasped, taking her first breath in too long.

"HUI I! W-W-WATSON!" she cried. "YOU ARE A ST-ST-STAR! YOU SAVED M-M-MY LIFE!"

"RUFF!" he agreed as she held him tight.

Then she looked up at the captain.

"And you-oo-oo have an extremely kn-kn-knobbly knee!"

He whipped off his hat and covered his knee with it.

"That's enough about my knee, Miss Dilys. What the blazes are you doing in here? You could have been killed."

"The s-s-s-spots of b-b-brandy led all the way d-d-down here."

"Oh! Not all this again! Chef murdered the Maestro and then leaped into the sea. End of story."

He heaved Dilly to her feet.

"It's not the end of the st-st-story," she replied. "It's just the b-b-beginning."

"What do you mean?"

"Chef never leaped into the sea. F-f-follow me."

The captain lit a match. Then he and Watson followed Dilly until they reached the end of the ice room.

There, still very frozen, and still very dead, was Chef.

"Oh my goodness!" gasped the captain.

"So, do you still think Chef murdered the Maestro?"

The captain was no fool. "No. He was murdered too."

"BINGO!"

"Was it the same person who murdered the Maestro?"

"I think so."

"Why?"

Dilly pulled her notebook from her snow-dusted satchel. She flicked to the right page.

"Look, there were three sets of feet involved in the struggle in the kitchen. The Maestro's. Chef's. And someone else's."

"Whose?"

"I don't know yet, but I do know the murderer is still on this ship. I was very nearly their third victim. Someone locked me in here."

"Oh no. Poor you. Did you catch a glimpse of them?"

"Only a silhouette. It was too misty. Before you burst in, I was moments from death."

"Well, thank goodness for Sherlock," he said, looking down at the dog.

"WATSON!" corrected Dilly. "I'm the Sherlock in this relationship."

"RUFF!"

"This clever little one dragged me all the way down from the bridge."

"He's the best," she replied, opening her satchel, and

throwing him another dog biscuit.

"WOOF!" he barked, catching it in his mouth.

Immediately, Watson spat it out as it was frozen solid.

SPUT!

"Now, let's get you out of here, Miss Dilys. And fast. Before the murderer strikes again!"

CHAPTER FOURTEEN

GROUNDED!

"Grounded?"

"YES! GROUNDED! WITH A CAPITAL 'GR'!"

Gladys was standing in Dilly's cabin with her arms folded. The girl had a blanket wrapped round her and was still shivering from the cold.

The captain shifted uneasily on his feet. He did not want to intrude on a family dispute.

"I will leave you two to it," he said, hurrying through the door.

"But, Auntie, me and Watson need to crack the case!"

This only enraged the woman further.

"ARE YOU BANANAS? YOU NEARLY GOT YOURSELF KILLED!"

"All the more reason to catch the murderer."

"RUFF!"

"No! I am not letting you out of this cabin and ruining the trip for me! Like you ruin everything!"

Dilly felt like bursting into tears. But she wasn't going to let this bully beat her.

"WHAT ABOUT WATSON?"

"What about Watson?"

"I need to walk him."

"You have been using that as an excuse to run amok!"

"But he needs to do his business."

"RUFF!"

"It's less than a week! He can hold it in!"

"HRUM!" Watson whimpered.

Fox popped his head round the door.

"Excuse me, but I heard raised voices. Is everything tickety-boo?"

"Oh, hello, my one true love. You won't believe it, but this silly sausage got herself locked in the ice room!"

Fox was astounded. "No! No! No! You poor thing!" he cried, giving her a much-needed hug.

Then he noticed his suit was damp. "You are wet through! Let me run you a steaming hot bath!"

"Thank you."

He smiled and edged past Gladys to the bathroom.

The soothing sound of water sploshing into a bath followed, before steam drifted into the cabin.

It was already warming Dilly up.

"I popped in some bath salts for you."

"Thank you."

"My pleasure! Shall we all go to luncheon when you are out of the bath?"

"No. Dilly is too scared to leave her cabin now."

"No, I'm not!"

"Yes, you are! So we won't see her again until we reach Southampton."

"But she'll starve, poor girl."

"We can slide a piece of toast under the cabin door. Now come on, Handsome!"

With that, she yanked Fox out.

A bath was the perfect place to think. Especially one as smooth and sumptuous as this. Back home in Wales, Dilly had only bathed in cold water in a battered old tin bath. Outside. It was more of a sheep dip, in fact.

This bath had gold taps and perfectly rounded porcelain.

"There is somewhere we haven't searched yet, Watson. Somewhere that may help us crack the case."

"RUFF?"

"The Maestro's cabin."

Watson nodded.

"There might be a clue or two in there. Let's go!"

So, after serving less than an hour of her prison sentence, Dilly had gone on the run. She did her best to disguise herself by pulling a cloth cap down over her eyes and stuffing Watson up her jumper.

He didn't like this one bit. But he was a dead giveaway. Dilly was the only passenger with a dog.

A sign on the door to the Maestro's cabin read:

ENTRY FORBIDDEN.

Of course, the door was locked. This was a job for Dilly's trusty paperclip. After a few seconds of waggling...

CLICK!

...she was inside, and she locked the door behind her.

The Maestro's cabin was the finest on

THE MASQUERADE. It was impossible to imagine anything swankier. Every inch was opulent.

The poor people (well, rich people) who had been thrown out of this cabin to make way for the Maestro must be FUMING!

Dilly set Watson down on a polar-bear rug.

His fur had gone funny when he was stuffed up her jumper.

EXHIBIT:

BEFORE JUMPER

AFTER JUMPER

He shook himself back to normal and began sniffing around the cabin for clues.

"We're looking for something, Watson. We just don't know what yet!"

"RUFF!"

A hunt through the mahogany drawers and cupboards unearthed nothing more than silk pyjamas, monogrammed velvet slippers and cashmere socks in every shade of red.

Dilly's eyes were drawn to a large red leather-bound book on the desk.

It was a diary, the finest money could buy. It had a gold **M** embossed in the bottom right-hand corner.

For an amateur sleuth like Dilly, this was the find of the century! The diary of the greatest detective/opera singer the world had ever known! A legend who had solved dozens of murders!

Though, sadly, not his own.

Her hands trembling with anticipation, she opened the book. She flicked through the pages until she found his final fateful entry.

Saturday 14th of December 1929

The Masquerade may be a hell hole with ghastly cabins, disgusting food and the most repulsive peasants on board, but it will soon be the scene of the greatest triumph of the Maestro's glittering career.

There is a face the Maestro recognised on board *The Masquerade*. A face of **evil**. The face of a cold-hearted **killer** who has thus far eluded the great Maestro, and all the lesser detectives that follow in his wake. Tonight, at the stroke of midnight, in the dining room, with an audience of hundreds, after enjoying his blancmange, the Maestro will finally unmask the **murderer!**

"Who? Who is this killer?" whispered Dilly.

Watson shook his head.

Just then she heard the doorhandle rattling.

Someone was about to burst in…!

CHAPTER FIFTEEN

UNDER A BLACK VEIL

"Watson!" whispered Dilly as she put the diary back in its place. "Here!"

The dog dashed towards his mistress. She grabbed him and together they hid under the four-poster bed. Lying on the floor, she could feel something sharp digging into her tummy.

After some more rattling of the doorhandle, Dilly heard the lock being picked.

Then...

CLICK!

The door was opened, then hurriedly closed again, behind whoever had just come in.

From their hiding place, Dilly and Watson could only spy a pair of lady's feet and the wheels of a bathchair. It seemed to be a woman pushing someone else in the chair.

The hem of a black satin dress dragged across the floor.

Who **were** these two?

Dilly and Watson didn't dare breathe.

The pair of interlopers wheeled round the cabin, until they stopped at the desk.

RIP!

A page was **ripped out** of the Maestro's diary.

Then there was the sound of a match being struck, and the glow of fire.

The bathroom door opened, and the burning page dropped into the toilet bowl. Then the chain was pulled, and the embers of the page were flushed out into the Atlantic Ocean.

A vital piece of evidence had been destroyed!

Meanwhile, Dilly slipped her hand underneath her tummy to retrieve the sharp object.

It was a cufflink with an **M** engraved on it.

It must be **M** for Maestro?

Or could it be **M** for Morosov, the Russian novelist?

Dilly placed it in her pocket. This was a vital piece of evidence.

The pair wheeled back over to the cabin door. Rattling the handle, one of them dropped something.

A hairpin. It must have been used to pick the lock. A black-gloved hand came down to pick it up. Hair hung down. Dilly saw the curve of a nose…

Oh no!

Were they about to be rumbled?

No, the figure snapped up again as soon as they had snared the hairpin. The door opened, and the pair passed through it faster than the Flying Scotsman!*

As soon as the door had closed, Dilly crawled out from under the bed, Watson at her heels. If she were fast enough, she might catch a glimpse of the intruder. She opened the door and peered through the crack.

---

* ONE OF THE FASTEST TRAINS IN THE WORLD. NOT AN ACTUAL SCOTSMAN WHO COULD FLY.

The lady seated on the bathchair looked like a widow at a funeral.

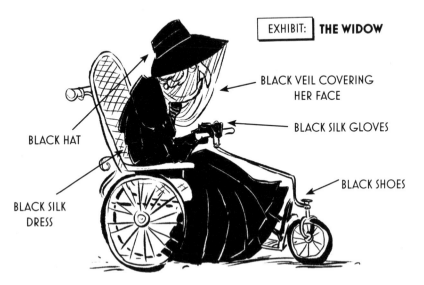

EXHIBIT: **THE WIDOW**

BLACK VEIL COVERING HER FACE

BLACK SILK GLOVES

BLACK HAT

BLACK SHOES

BLACK SILK DRESS

The lady pushing the bathchair was a nurse. She was pushing the Black Widow so fast that she was about to collide with the Hungarian professor, who was coming down the corridor in the other direction.

"STOP!" he shouted.

THWUCK!

The professor was hurled into the air. And landed in a jumble of limbs on the floor.

DOOF!

"NO!" he cried. "IT'S YOU!"

The widow's veil had come off in the collision. She quickly put it back on and barked at him in Norwegian.

"*Flytt deg, din fordømte idiot.*"

Then the silent nurse pushed her round a corner.

And she was gone.

Dilly was in turmoil.

Should she chase after them?

Or stop and help the professor?

The old man groaned...

"URGH!"

...and she knew she had to do the right thing.

Watson leaped on the professor's chest and began licking his face.

"SLURP!"

The man was revived instantly.

"WHA—!"

"Don't worry, Professor. It's just my partner in crime, Watson."

Dilly sat him up and noticed he had a big bump on his forehead.

"You poor man. Does it hurt?" she asked, pressing it with her finger.

"OW! It hurts like crazy when you touch it!"

"Sorry! Shall I call the doctor?"

"No! No! No! I don't trust doctors. Just please help me back to my cabin."

As she did so, Dilly asked, "Did you get a close look at her?"

"Yes."

"What did she look like?"

"Well, this might seem strange, especially to you, but…"

"But what?"

"Eurgh! I'm feeling very dizzy!"

Dilly made the dazed and confused professor comfortable in his cabin. Then left him there for now. She would be back as soon as he'd had a chance to gather his thoughts – right now, she needed to chase after the mysterious pair who had broken into the Maestro's cabin.

However, as soon as Dilly had taken a few steps from the door, she heard a thud from inside.

THWUMP!

She rushed back to the door, but it was locked.

"Professor? Are you all right?"

"I am fine, child!" came the reply, in that strong Hungarian accent of his.

"I heard something. It sounded like you fell."

"No! Just me slumping down on my bed."

"Can I help with anything?"

"No, no, child. I just need to rest!"

"If you are sure."

"I am sure. Now run along back to your cabin and don't forget to lock the door!"

"I won't," lied Dilly.

CHAPTER SIXTEEN

WAKE THE DEAD

Try as they might, Dilly and Watson could find no sign of the mysterious widow in the bathchair, or the nurse pushing her.

So, instead, they went in search of **THE MASQUERADE'S** mortuary. There, Dilly could check if the Maestro was missing a cufflink monogrammed with the letter **M.** If he was, then she could discount it as a clue. A good detective never jumps to conclusions.

The mortuary was difficult to find.

Dilly could hardly ask for directions.

"Excuse me, please can you kindly tell me the way to the mortuary?"

It was far below deck, where passengers never ventured. Unless they were dead. And then they were allowed to enter. No problem. Come on in and make yourself at home! Relax!

After snaking around the maze of gangways, and taking wrong turns to dead ends, Dilly found a metal door.

A sign read: **MORTUARY.** There was no **DO NOT ENTER** sign, but there didn't need to be.

Who else other than Dilly would dare venture inside?

Listening out for footsteps, Dilly picked the lock with her trusty paperclip.

CLICK!

She found the light switch.

SNAP!

A bulb dangling from the ceiling flickered on.

The mortuary emerged from the gloom.

There was a huge marble slab in the centre. This must be where the bodies were laid to be examined. There were also:

SHELVES STOCKED WITH BOTTLES OF EMBALMING FLUID

A PILE OF WHITE SHEETS

A SQUARE SIN ON A STAND

A LAUNDRY BASKET

All along the back wall was a floor-to-ceiling cabinet. There were a dozen drawers where bodies were stored.

THE MASQUERADE had only been at sea for a few days, but there were already two dead bodies on board. The Maestro and Chef.

Her heart pounding, Dilly and Watson tiptoed to the cabinet. It was unnecessary to be this quiet, as there was no chance of waking anyone up. Still, the mortuary was seriously eerie, so it felt like the right thing to do.

She didn't want to wake the dead.

A TROLLEY OF
MEDICAL INSTRUMENTS

Most of the drawers were blank, but two were labelled with names.

Dilly found the one marked "Maestro".

She pulled on the drawer, and after a sticky start it rolled out. The body was covered in a white sheet, like a ghost taking a snooze.

"HUH!" she gasped.

It was **not** a pretty sight. The blancmange had dried and gone crusty. The Maestro's face looked like a killer clown's.

Dilly dropped the sheet on the floor, then checked the cuffs of the Maestro's shirt. Both cuffs had cufflinks. Cufflinks that were infinitely more ornate than the one Dilly had found under his bed. Cufflinks that were encrusted with diamonds.

"This cufflink doesn't look like one of his!" whispered Dilly, comparing the two. "Perhaps it is Morosov's?"

"RUFF!" agreed Watson.

"That would make sense."

The next drawer along was marked "CHEF".

Icy water leaked out of it and on to the floor, causing a huge puddle that was spreading fast. Dilly pulled open the drawer and double-checked it was him.

Now that Chef was thawing out, she spotted something. He had the imprint of a whisk on his forehead!

"So, it wasn't Chef who'd used the whisk as a weapon! Someone used it on him!"

Then Watson burst into life. "WOOF! WOOF! WOOF!"

"Not now, Watson! I need to think."

"WOOF! WOOF! WOOF!"

Dilly spun round to see if there was anyone at the door.

"WOOF! WOOF! WOOF!" barked Watson, running round in circles. Then he tapped his paw against another drawer, which was open a chink.

Dilly pulled out the drawer.

There was a third body!

"HUH!"

Dilly took a deep breath, then picked up the edge of the sheet.

But, just as she was about to reveal who was underneath, the body sat up!

"ARGH!" screamed Dilly.

"WOOF!"

Dilly scooped Watson up and bolted towards the door, slipping and sliding on the wet floor.

WHOOSH!

She fell face first, almost crushing Watson, who was in her arms.

"ARGH!"

"WOOF!"

Dilly tried to drag herself to the door.

"HELP!" she screamed.

She rolled over on to her back to see who or what was pursuing her. A figure, partially concealed by a white sheet, had leaped out of the drawer. Now it was chasing her, arms outstretched!

"DON'T KILL ME! PLEASE!" she pleaded.
Pale hands reached out to grab her.
"NOₒₒOOOOOOOₒOOOOOₒOOₒₒO
OₒOOOOOOOOₒₒₒOOOO!"

ACT III

DEATH BY BEARD

CHAPTER SEVENTEEN

DEEPER AND DARKER

As Dilly scrambled away from the outstretched hands, Watson barked and barked and barked at this terrifying figure.

"WOOF! WOOF! WOOF!"

He bit on to the end of the sheet that covered them.

CHOMP!

Whoever was under there didn't want to be seen. They tried to boot the dog away.

BOF! BOF! BOF!

But Watson was not giving up. He yanked on the sheet to reveal…

THE BLACK WIDOW!

Clearly, she didn't need that bathchair, after all!

A flurry of kicks was unleashed.

One of them found its target!

THWOD!

Poor Watson was sent spinning across the mortuary floor.

WHOOZZ!

"YOW!"

He curled up into a ball and Dilly caught him.

The Black Widow turned round and picked up the sheet. She spun the sheet round and round itself, forming it into a long, twisted rope. Then she cracked it like a whip.

CRACK!

She whipped the sheet at the ceiling, smashing the lightbulb.

SMASH!

Now the mortuary was plunged into darkness.

Then, still brandishing the "whip" she paced towards Dilly and Watson, her heeled shoes tapping on the damp floor.

TAP! TAP! TAP!

Dilly was still holding Watson, who was shaking with fear. She did the only sensible thing there was to do.

SHE RAN!

SHE RAN FOR HER LIFE!

AND SHE RAN FOR WATSON'S LIFE!

They raced out of the mortuary, slamming the door behind them.

THWUNT!

They sped along the gangway.

Up flight after flight of steps.

Not stopping.

Not looking back.

Not pausing for breath.

TERROR, DREAD and FEAR made Dilly's heart beat faster, powering her legs.

RUN! RUN! RUN!

THE MASQUERADE was reeling from side to side in the storm.

Dilly and Watson stumbled as they were hurled against the walls.

She needed to tell the captain what had just happened.

But, striding up the steps to the deck, she spied her aunt's brand-new shoes on the way down.

DISASTER!

One more step and Gladys would see that, despite her orders, Dilly was out of her cabin.

So Dilly spun and ran back down the stairs. There was every chance that her aunt was going to check on her, so she raced to her cabin.

She flung herself inside and shut the door behind her.

Then there was a pounding on the door.

KNOCK! KNOCK! KNOCK!

Dilly didn't dare breathe.

KNOCK! KNOCK! KNOCK!

It must be the Black Widow!

KNOCK! KNOCK! KNOCK!

Then Dilly heard a voice.

"OPEN THIS DOOR, YOU LITTLE WORM!"

Reluctantly, Dilly opened the door. Auntie Gladys entered, humming the "Wedding March".

"BUM! BUM! BUM! BUM! BUMMPETY BUM!"

Dilly stared. Her heart still pounding with fear, it took her a while to realise that her aunt was full of...

JOY!

Gladys twirled around the cabin, holding on to her invisible dance partner.

It was hard to work out if she were tottering because of the storm or because she'd had a few drinks.

"GUESS!" she said.

"Guess what?"

"GUESS!"

"WHAT?"

"JUST GUESS!"

"I don't know what I am guessing!"

"Guess what just happened!"

"I don't know!"

"Foxy **proposed!**"

Dilly and Watson shared a look.

"Wow," said Dilly. "That was quick!"

"He had to snap me up before some other lucky blighter got there first. Oh! It was sooooo romantic! He got down on one knee on the deck as we watched dawn rise. Not someone called Dawn rise, but—"

"I know what you meant."

"And look at this big sparkler!"

On her finger was a ring with the biggest diamond you could ever imagine.

"I am getting married. To a lord. I'll be rich!"

"You are already rich."

"Oh yes! Of course I am! **Stinking rich!** But now I'll have all of what's his, *and* I'll be a lady."

"Lucky guy!" Dilly said sarcastically. "So where is he?"

"Why? What's your wicked little plan?"

"I don't have one. I just wanted to tell him, well, congratulations, and—"

"His lordship is too busy to talk to the likes of you! He dashed off to send a telegram to his old mum who is a duchess or something to share the joyful news! Oh! And guess—"

"Not this again."

"Just guess!"

"Guess what?"

"Guess when we are getting married!"

"Oh, erm, next year?"

"No."

"Next month?"

"No."

"Next week?"

"NO!"

"I don't know."

"GUESS!"

"Just tell me!"

"Tomorrow!"

"Tomorrow? But we'll still be at sea tomorrow."

"We're getting married on the ship, DIMBO!"

"Don't you need a priest to get married?"

"No! A captain can do it! We're gonna celebrate now in the champagne bar!"

"Can I come to the wedding?"

"What, and be a bridesmaid?"

"If you like."

"NO! I am not having an ugly duckling like you ruining my big day. You will stay shut up here!"

Then Gladys narrowed her eyes and stared at her niece.

"Why are you sweating like a pig?"

"Am I?"

"YES!" she snapped, stalking over to her and feeling her brow. "You are all hot and sweaty! WHERE HAVE YOU BEEN?"

"Nowhere."

Watson nodded to back up the lie. He was hot and drooling.

"So why are you all hot and sweaty, then?"

Dilly didn't answer.

"I asked you a question!"

"Guess!" replied Dilly, buying time to think.

"I do not play stupid guessing games! You tell me right now why you are all hot and sweaty or I will give you a good thrashing!"

"Er, well, um, it's because it's boiling in here."

"IT'S NOT!"

"It was."

"WHEN?"

"Just before you came in! Then it cooled down."

"HOW?"

"I opened the porthole."

Gladys stalked over to the little round window. "THE PORTHOLES DON'T OPEN!"

"It did a moment ago."

Gladys was becoming increasingly suspicious. "Don't you forget you are grounded for the rest of the trip! Do you hear me, you lying little toad? GROUNDED!"

"But I need to talk to the captain right away! It's a matter of life and death."

"I don't want to hear another word out of you until we reach Southampton!"

"But—"

"I'VE GOT A GOOD MIND TO LOCK YOU IN THE CUPBOARD!"

"GRRR!" growled Watson.

"AND YOU, YOU STINKY LITTLE MUTT!" she shouted, before stomping across the cabin and slamming the door behind her.

SHUNT!

An oil painting fell off the wall.

THWUMP!

With her aunt on the warpath, Dilly had no choice but to sit tight for a moment.

She dragged a chair to the door and jammed it under the handle.

That way, if she managed to get out of the mortuary, the murderous widow couldn't force her way in.

Then Dilly sat on her bed.

Her life was in grave danger. And she couldn't even tell her aunt.

Since the woman had inherited that ton of cash, she had become worse, if that were possible. Meaner. Crueler. Nastier.

All Auntie Gladys had ever wanted was to be rich. But now that she was, she wanted to be even richer! She didn't love Fox. She just loved his money.

However, Fox was the best thing to have happened to Dilly in her short life. He was as kind to her as Gladys allowed him to be. But she was a bully and she would bully Fox. In the end, Gladys was going to get her own way and rid herself of her niece forever, even though Dilly had nowhere else to go. The house had been sold, so she couldn't go back there. Besides, she was too young to be allowed to live alone.

It would be the orphanage.

And she would never see Watson again. He would be put in the dog pound. And no dogs ever got out of there alive.

She was going to lose her only friend in the world. The thought was unbearable. A tear rolled down her cheek. It felt futile crying for herself, but no one else would.

And, as if all this wasn't nightmarish enough, there was still a murderer at large – a double murderer – and Dilly was the only one trying to solve the case. All the grown-ups did was get in the way.

Every time she came closer to unravelling the mystery, it deepened and darkened. Just who was this weird widow, and why did she want Dilly dead?

If Dilly didn't unmask this murderer fast, there would be more dead bodies. Including hers!

It was turning into a HORROR STORY.

Just then, Watson barked.

"WOOF!"

"What is it, Watson?"

"WOOF! WOOF! WOOF!"

Watson had leaped on to the desk and had his nose pressed up against the porthole.

The storm had worsened, and a mighty wave struck the glass.

SPLOOSH!

It was only when the water ran down that Dilly could see what all the barking was about.

An aeroplane was circling overhead.

"We are in the middle of the Atlantic Ocean. What is a plane doing all the way out here?"

But, before Watson could answer, someone leaped out of it!

CHAPTER EIGHTEEN

A CAT-SIZED PARACHUTE

When Dilly reached the deck, she was relieved to see a parachute had opened. Whoever was dangling from the parachute was battling the wind and rain to try to land on the deck of THE MASQUERADE.

Then another figure leaped from the plane.

A much smaller figure.

"A CAT!" cried Dilly.

"WOOF!" barked Watson, running round in circles, trying to find the cat.

"UP THERE!" Dilly said, pointing.

Above the ship, a little cat-sized parachute* opened, with a cat dangling underneath.

Watson started leaping up on his hind legs to get closer to the cat.

"GRRRR!"

"Calm down, boy!"

---

* A CATACHUTE.

As the parachuting pair neared **THE MASQUERADE**, Dilly recognised them.

"FRAU Fröhlich!" she cried. "AND KINSKI THE CAT!"

Frau Fröhlich was an elderly German detective, Kinski her cat companion.

EXHIBIT:

KINSKI

RUBY-RED LIPSTICK

LEATHER GLOVES

BERET

GOGGLES

FANGS

TIE

PLATINUM-BLONDE HAIR

CIGARETTE HOLDER

COLLAR

TURTLENECK JUMPER

TAIL THAT CRACKS LIKE A WHIP. **SNAP!**

TWEED SUIT

RAZOR-SHARP CLAWS

BOOTS

EXHIBIT:

FRAU FRÖHLICH

All Fröhlich's triumphs were collected in a series of celebrated casebooks:

- **LOST IN THE BLACK FOREST (GATEAUX)**
- **OOM-PAH-PAHED TO DEATH**
- **THE MYSTERY OF THE MISSING ZEPPELIN**
- **THE CURIOUS CASE OF THE LEDERHOSEN WEDGIE**
- **THE WURST BRATWURST**
- **THE CUCKOO CLOCK OF HORROR**
- **THE SECRET CODE OF BEETHOVEN'S BEER BURPS**
- **THE HAUNTED ACCORDION**
- **ESCAPE FROM ONIONFEST**
- **SCHNITZELLED!**

But, as she watched, Dilly realised something was going badly wrong. The storm was blowing Fröhlich and her cat way off course.

They were going to overshoot the ship and plunge into the cruel sea!

Any moment now, Fröhlich was facing a catastrophe. And her cat a catcatastrophe.

Passengers and crew stretched out their

arms to try to grab them as they sailed over their heads. But no one could reach.

"*HÉLFEN! HÉLFEN! IDIOTEN!*"

Dilly rushed towards the stern. Spotting a tall pile of deckchairs, she climbed to the top. Then she launched herself at Fröhlich's ankles.

"*AUTSCH!*" yelled the lady.

"GOT YOU!" cried Dilly.

Meanwhile, Watson launched himself at Kinski, biting on to the cat's tail.

CHOMP!

"YEOW!"

But, even with the added weight, they were not descending fast enough.

"*NEIN! NEIN!*"

Now there could be no doubt. They were going to overshoot the ship.

At the very end of **THE MASQUERADE** stood a flagpole.

Dilly steered her and Fröhlich towards it. And, just as she was about to hit the flagpole, she stretched out her legs and wrapped them round it.

"PARACHUTE!" Dilly shouted.

Fröhlich detached it and the wind swept it into the ocean.

With her free hand, Dilly grabbed hold of Watson's tail.

The weight of all four at the top of the flagpole forced it to bend.

TWONG!.

It bent forward and then snapped back.

TWANG!

They were catapulted backwards.

WHOOSH!

"*NEIN!*"

"NO!"

"WOOF!"

"YEOW!"

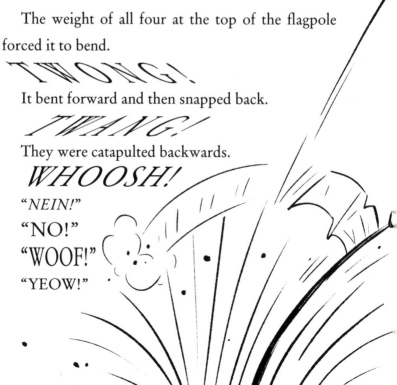

WHIZZ!!!

The four flew backwards and hit a funnel.

CLONK! CLONK! CLONK! CLONK!

They slid down the funnel, landing in a heap on the deck.

If Dilly were expecting to be thanked for saving Frau Fröhlich's life, she was disappointed.

"YOU STUPID *IDIOTEN!*" shouted the lady as she shoved the girl off her.

The captain helped Fröhlich to her feet as the cat sank her fangs into Watson's tail in revenge.

"RRROOOUUUCCCHHH!" he yelped.

"Frau Fröhlich, it's an honour to have you aboard **THE MASQUERADE**," began the captain.

"PAH!"

"And, Dilly, thank you for saving our esteemed guest's life."

Dilly beamed. Watson leaped up into her arms to escape from the cat, who was circling menacingly.

" **HISS!** "

"I couldn't let the great detective drown," said Dilly.

Frau Fröhlich was fuming, however. "I did not need rescuing! I know how to swim and would have easily caught up with the ship!"

Dilly and the captain shared a look of disbelief.

"Well, what about your cat?" she asked.

"Kinski is a champion swimmer!"

"Really?"

"*JA!* She won gold in backstroke at the Cat Olympics! Now, please, let me get down to business!"

"So, you received my telegram, Frau Fröhlich?" asked the captain.

"Such tragical news about the Maestro," the lady said with a wicked grin. It was clear she'd loathed him. "Now I, Frau Fröhlich, am the world's greatest detective!"

"Thank goodness you are here," said Dilly. "I was about to tell the captain that someone just tried to kill me!"

"Who? When? Where?" he asked.

"Follow me!" Dilly said. "And I'll show you."

"Where is this *Kind* taking us?" asked Fröhlich.

Dilly turned, enjoying the drama. "To the mortuary!"

CHAPTER NINETEEN

ANOTHER DEAD BODY

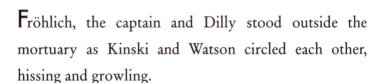

Fröhlich, the captain and Dilly stood outside the mortuary as Kinski and Watson circled each other, hissing and growling.

"HISS!"

"GRRR!"

Fröhlich was about to open the door when Dilly put her hand on it to stop her.

"Wait," she said.

"*Herr Kapitän*! You need to control this *Kind*!"

"I have tried."

"The murderer might have gone back inside," said Dilly. "We should be careful."

"Who *is* it?" the captain asked.

"It was the Black Widow."

"The who?" said Fröhlich.

"A Norwegian lady dressed in black. She was the one

who tried to kill me in there."

"Convenient to be murdered in a mortuary," replied Fröhlich. "As soon as you are dead, you can open a drawer and climb inside. Save someone else the bother."

"And you think this widow killed both the victims?" asked the captain.

"I don't know," said Dilly. "But she certainly tried to kill me."

"We must enter and investigate!" said Frau Fröhlich.

"Yes," said the captain. "Now, where is the key?"

He searched his bunch, but before he could find the right key Dilly picked the lock with her paperclip.

CLICK!

"Why, thank you, Miss Dilys," he huffed.

"All in a day's work, Captain."

"Ladies," he said, "stand aside. I will go first."

"Sexist *Schwein*!" snapped Fröhlich. "I will go first!"

Fröhlich took a torch out of her handbag, pushed the others aside and stepped into the darkness.

"So where is this killer widow of yours now, *Kind*?" purred Fröhlich, pointing the beam of light into the dark, damp corners of the mortuary.

"I don't know. Maybe she is hiding."

"If she was ever here at all, that is. Now where is the Maestro?"

"In here," replied the captain, pulling out the drawer. Fröhlich examined him.

"Oh yes! He's dead all right. Killed by blancmange! It's what he would have wanted. Was the blancmange poisoned?"

"Not as far as anyone could tell. It looked like he drowned in it."

"He never was a strong swimmer like me or Kinski. And blancmange is difficult to swim in. Now, where is the chief murder suspect – the chef?"

"He's in here!" replied Dilly, opening the drawer.

"At first we all believed, well, apart from Miss Dilys here, that Chef had murdered the Maestro," said the captain. "But then we found him dead inside a huge block of ice."

"In his *Unterhosen*?"

The captain nodded.

"Could he have climbed inside this block of ice?"

"It seems unlikely," replied Dilly.

"I was asking *Herr Kapitän*!"

"It seems unlikely."

"That is what I thought. Suspicious. Very suspicious."

Dilly retraced her steps from earlier. "I think the Black Widow was hiding in here," she replied, touching a drawer.

"RUFF!" agreed Watson.

Fröhlich smirked and shook her head, resting her hand on the handle. "Ha! Ha! And now, of course, it is empty!"

With a sense of theatrics, Fröhlich pulled open the drawer without even looking.

"SEE! EMPTY!"

But it wasn't. There was a body lying under a sheet.

"Frau Fröhlich," said the captain.

"*Ja?*"

"There is actually a dead body in there."

"ARGH!" she screamed, jumping away and landing on her cat.

" M M M I I A A O O O W W W ! "

She dropped the torch, which Watson retrieved with his mouth.

"Why didn't you tell me?" she demanded.

"I did! Stand back, ladies. This must be the Black Widow."

He whisked off the sheet.

"Strange-looking lady," said Fröhlich, illuminating the figure's face with her torch. "She has a very long beard! WHO IS THIS?"

"It's the professor!" exclaimed Dilly.

"What could he have to do with all this?" asked the captain.

"I only just saw him," said Dilly. "He was run down by the widow in her bathchair, and I helped him back to his cabin."

"Suspicious!" said Fröhlich. "Very suspicious."

"How did he die?" spluttered the captain.

Fröhlich shone her torch on the old man's face. His eyes were bulging and his tongue was sticking out of his mouth. As for his long beard, that was wrapped tightly round his own neck!

"Strangled by his own beard!" she proclaimed.

CHAPTER TWENTY

INTERROGATION

Within moments, Fröhlich had set up an interrogation room in the ship's library.

There she grilled everyone on board that she considered a suspect.

Passengers.

Crew.

Even the captain.

Last, she summoned Dilly. The girl was waiting outside the library as the captain emerged. He looked like a naughty schoolboy who had just been punished by his headmaster.

"Good luck, Miss Dilys," he croaked, his mouth as dry as a desert. "You will need it."

"COME!" called Fröhlich.

Dilly immediately glowed bright red with guilt, even though she was one hundred per cent innocent. She stepped into the library, Watson at her heels.

"NO *HUNDS* IN HERE!" barked Fröhlich.

"RUFF!" he protested.

"OUT!"

Still, Watson stood his ground. There was never a more loyal dog.

Kinski was crouched on top of a bookcase.

" HISS ! "

She launched herself at the dog.

Fangs ready to bite.

Claws ready to scratch.

Paws ready to punch.

Tail ready to whip.

Whiskers ready to tickle.

Such was the speed of the attack, or rather CATATTACK, poor Watson didn't stand a chance.

Kinski landed on top of the dog, knocking him off his paws.

"RUFF!"

Watson fell on to his back, his legs waggling in the air, like an upside-down beetle.

With one whip of her tail, Kinski sent him flying across the floor.

SNAP!

WHOOSH!

He shot out of the library, before the cat slammed the door after him.

S H U N T !

Watson whimpered outside.

"HUMM! HUMM!"

Dilly spun round to go to him, but Fröhlich ordered:

"SIT!"

Dilly sat.

As you might imagine of a library, it was full of books.*

Beautiful old leatherbound books. In deep reds, rich greens and sombre blacks. Hundreds, if not thousands of them. Weighted with words.

At the centre of the room was a huge, detailed model of **THE MASQUERADE**. It was as long as Dilly was tall. As was tradition with model ships, it was housed in a bottle – in this case, a giant one.

Fröhlich was sitting at an imposing wooden desk, her chair like a throne. Dilly was sitting on a footstool. That was no accident; it was so Fröhlich could loom over her murder suspects, intimidating them.

---

* NONE OF MINE. AND CERTAINLY NOT THIS ONE BECAUSE, AS OF NOW, I AM STILL WRITING IT.

The stool was so low that Dilly's knees reached her chin. She might as well have sat on the floor.

"How can I help, Frau Fröhlich?" asked Dilly in the chirpiest tone she could muster.

Kinski stalked over to the desk and leaped on to it. She slunk across it, her bottom dangerously close to her mistress's nose.

"*KINSKI! NEIN!*" said Frau Fröhlich, sweeping her away.

The cat leaped up on to a bookcase.

"So, Dilly, if that even is your real name…"

"It's Dilys."

"Dilly! Dilys! Whatever your name is, please explain why **you,** and you alone, have just happened to be at the scene of every murder?"

Dilly gulped. This was terrifying. One wrong word and she could spend the rest of her life in prison!

The questions came thick and fast like bullets from a machine gun.

RAT! TAT! TAT!

So fast that it was impossible to think, let alone answer.

"Why were your footprints found in the kitchen where the Maestro was murdered?"

"Well, I... er—"

"What were you doing in the Maestro's *Kabine*?"

"How do you know—"

"Why was a page ripped out of his diary?"

"It wasn't me—"

"Then **who** was it?"

"Please let me explain—"

"Yes, please do explain why your grubby little *Fingerabdrücke* were found on his diary?"

"Fingerprints?"

"*JA! FINGERABDRÜCKE!*"

"Because I needed to—"

"Why did you steal the *Manschettenknopf*?"

"The what?"

"The cufflink!"

"How do you know I took a cufflink?"

"I had your *Kabine* searched, and it was found in your satchel!"

Frau Fröhlich lifted it from the desk.

"I didn't steal it; it's a clue…"

"A clue that damns you! Why did you make up this ridiculous *russisch* novelist?"

"Morosov? I didn't make him up! His books must be in here somewhere! Under M."

Fröhlich rolled her eyes as Dilly rushed over to a shelf in the library, only to find nothing by Morosov.

"I already checked, you *Dummkopf*! You invented Morosov to create a false alibi for your murder of the *Chefkoch*, didn't you?"

"That is not true! I swear on my life!"

"Your life will be worth nothing!"

"What?"

"You will spend the rest of it behind bars! Because

179

that was just the beginning!"

"The beginning of what?"

"Your murder spree!"

"NO!"

"Why did you break your poor auntie's order for the grounding?"

"I had to—"

"Do you always sneak off in the middle of the *Nacht*?"

"No, well, yes..."

"You were the last person to see the professor alive, weren't you?"

"Yes! But that doesn't mean—"

"What was your business in the mortuary? Was it to ensure there were no clues on your murder victims? Who are you planning to murder next? Is it me, because I am on to you? That's why the bodies have piled up, isn't it? So you can escape justice! *Nein!* I, Frau Fröhlich, will ensure you will be left to rot in prison! With only your *Hund* to eat!"

This tickled Kinski, who snickered.

"HISS! HISS!"

Silence descended on the library like snow. Fröhlich

glared at the girl, who was so beaten down she looked as if she were about to burst into tears.

"Well, *Fräulein*? What do you have to say for yourself?"

"Please, please, please let me explain—"

"Like everyone else, you have had your chance to explain!"

"Do you do this to everybody?"

"I need to see who cracks under pressure!"

"Did I crack? I mean, do you really think I did it?"

Fröhlich smiled. "You and all the other suspects are ordered to return here to the library at the stroke of *Mitternacht*! Then, and only then, will I unmask the KILLER!"

CHAPTER TWENTY-ONE

INSIDE THE CAPTAIN'S BRAIN

For the next few hours, Dilly sat stewing in her cabin. The only chance she had of proving her innocence to Frau Fröhlich was to find the killer herself. However, the case was still confounding her. So much of it didn't make sense.

Three dead bodies AND three mysterious characters:

1. Morosov the Russian novelist: an eyewitness who lied about what he saw.

2. The Brigadier: seen entering the kitchen just before the Maestro was found dead in the blancmange.

3. The Black Widow: sneaked into the Maestro's cabin with her nurse and burned the man's final diary entry. If that wasn't enough, she'd tried to kill Dilly and Watson in the mortuary.

Dilly needed to find all three suspects.

However, it was impossible, because, all this time, Auntie Gladys was sitting in the rocking cabin, keeping her beady eye on her.

"Auntie?"

"What?" From the woman's tone it seemed that whatever her niece was about to ask, the answer would be no.

"Please can I just pop out for a minute to walk Watson?"

"No."

"WHY?"

"RUFF?" added Watson.

"Because you are grounded!"

"Watson isn't grounded."

"RUFF!"

"You are both grounded!"

There was a tap on the door.

KNOCK!

"NOT TODAY, THANK YOU!" called Gladys.

KNOCK! KNOCK! KNOCK!

"It is me, my love!" called Fox from the other side of the door.

"FOXY!" cooed Gladys, rushing to the door, opening it and giving him a BIG SLOPPY KISS.

"Steady on," he said.

"One more sleep and we'll be man and wife!"

"A dream come true!"

"More a nightmare," muttered Dilly under her breath.

"WHAT DID YOU SAY?" demanded Gladys.

"Nothing!"

"Now, is there anything I can fetch you both? Tea? Scones? Cakes?" asked Fox.

"Ooh!" replied Dilly. "Can I have a banana milkshake, please?"

"No!" said Gladys. "Greedy pig! Just a bottle of champagne for me!"

A little later, after guzzling an entire bottle of champagne, Gladys was tipsy. Despite her best efforts, she couldn't keep her eyes open. Soon, she keeled over on the sofa and began snoring loudly.

"ZZZ! ZZZZ! ZZZZZ!"

Dilly knew this was her only chance! She tiptoed out of her cabin, Watson at her heels.

It was dark.

Midnight was drawing near.

She had to act fast.

The captain had mentioned the passenger list. That would be the best way of finding out which cabins the brigadier or the Black Widow might be in. So, she needed to sneak into the captain's study to find the log.

It was late. **THE MASQUERADE** was quiet. Most of the passengers and crew were in bed.

Dilly passed a few stragglers stumbling to their cabins after a night of eating, drinking and dancing.

The captain's study was located just behind the bridge. Dilly and Watson braved the wind and rain battering the deck to find it. Hiding in the shadows, so the captain and crew didn't spot her, she found the right door.

CAPTAIN'S STUDY
PLEASE KNOCK BEFORE ENTERING.

Of course, the door was locked, but that's what paperclips are made for. This trick never let her down.

CLICK!

The study was like being inside the captain's brain.

Instantly, Dilly felt at home here. But there wasn't time to sit down and make herself a mug of Bovril. There was work to be done.

She set the heavy book of passenger lists down on the desk and began leafing through it.

EXHIBIT: **PASSENGER LISTS**

NAME OF SHIP *The Masquerade* DAT

PORT OF DEPARTURE *New York*

NAMES OF

(1) TICKET NUMBER	(2) NAME
1011	Crompton, Richmal
1012	Dalí, Salvador
1013	de Lempicka, Tamar
1014	Disney, Walt
1015	Earhart, Amelia
1016	Einstein, Albert
1017	Ellington, Duke
1018	Fairbanks, Douglas
1019	Fields, W. C.
1020	Fitzgerald, F. Scott
1021	Ford, Henry
1022	Fox, Frederick (Lor

NAME OF SHIP *The Masquerade* DATE O

PORT OF DEPARTURE *New York*

NAMES OF PA

(1) TICKET NUMBER	(2) NAME
1001	Armstrong, Louis
1002	Baker, Josephine
1003	Beaton, Cecil
1004	Chanel, Coco
1005	Chaplin, Charlie
1006	Christie, Agatha
1007	Churchill, Winston
1008	Cocteau, Jean
1009	Cooper, Patience
1010	Coward, Noël

NAME OF SHIP _The Masquerade_   DATE OF DEPARTURE _Friday 13th December 1929_

PORT OF DEPARTURE _New York_   WHERE BOUND _Southampton_

NAMES OF PASSENGERS

(1) TICKET NUMBER	(2) NAME	(3) NATIONALITY	(4) ADDRESS
1023	Garbo, Greta		
1024	Gershwin, George		
1025	Gish, Lillian		
1026	Hayakawa, Sessue		
1027	Hoover, Herbert		
1028	Hughes, Langston		
1029	Jolson, Al		
1030	Kahlo, Frida		
1031	Keaton, Buster		
1032	Kulthum, Umm		
1033	Laurel, Stan		
1034	Lawrence, Gertrude		
1035	Lloyd George, David		
1036	Madoc, Dilys		
1037	Madoc, Gladys		
1038	O'Keeffe, Georgia		
1039	Picasso, Pablo		
1040	Professor, The		
1041	Rachmaninoff, Sergei		

NAME OF SHIP _The Masquerade_   DATE

PORT OF DEPARTURE _New York_

NAMES OF PA

(1) TICKET NUMBER	(2) NAME
1042	Rathbone, Basil
1043	Ruth, Babe
1044	Shostakovich, Dimitri
1045	Smith, Bessie
1046	Stravinsky, Igor
1047	Swanson, Gloria
1048	Tennant, Stephen
1049	Torres-García, Joaquín
1050	Wharton, Edith
1051	Woolf, Virginia
1052	Wong, Anna May
1053	Wray, Fay

The list was alphabetical, so Dilly turned straight to the Ms.

"The captain was right! No Morosov!"

"RUFF!" agreed Watson.

There was no one listed with the title of "Brigadier" either.

"Another person not on the list! Now what about the Black Widow? I have no idea of her name. But she's Norwegian. And the Norwegian alphabet looks a little different from the English one!"

EXHIBIT:

NORWEGIAN ALPHABET

A	B	C	D	E	F	G	H
a	b	c	d	e	f	g	h
I	J	K	L	M	N	O	P
i	j	k	l	m	n	o	p
Q	R	S	T	U	V	W	X
q	r	s	t	u	v	w	x
Y	Z	Æ	Ø	Å			
y	z	æ	ø	å			

As hard as she searched, Dilly couldn't find a single name with Norwegian letters.

She looked up at the clocks on the walls. The first one was about to reach midnight.

"Watson, we must run! No dillydallying for Dilly!"

Frau Fröhlich was minutes away from unmasking the killer.

And Dilly was praying it wasn't going to be her!

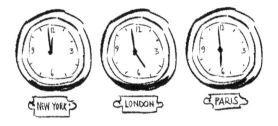

CHAPTER TWENTY-TWO

A MACABRE SIGHT

As Dilly and Watson neared the library, the door swung open. A bald man with a bushy moustache stumbled out. He wore dark glasses and held a long white stick, which he scratched across the floor in front of him. He was heading straight for her!

"Clear my path!"

He spoke with an Icelandic accent.

"Excuse me, sir?" said Dilly.

"Who is it?"

"My name is Dilly."

"Dilly?"

"Yes!"

"I am Magnus Magnus. Perhaps you have heard of me?"

"Sorry. I haven't."

"You shall. Magnus Magnus Magnus. Magnus is

my middle name also. I am Iceland's premier classical composer."

"I just don't know a thing about classical music."

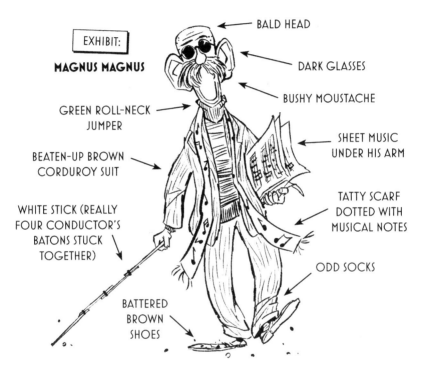

EXHIBIT:

MAGNUS MAGNUS

BALD HEAD

DARK GLASSES

BUSHY MOUSTACHE

GREEN ROLL-NECK JUMPER

SHEET MUSIC UNDER HIS ARM

BEATEN-UP BROWN CORDUROY SUIT

TATTY SCARF DOTTED WITH MUSICAL NOTES

WHITE STICK (REALLY FOUR CONDUCTOR'S BATONS STUCK TOGETHER)

ODD SOCKS

BATTERED BROWN SHOES

"Of course, and you are but... Let me guess... twelve?"

"Yes! How did you know?"

"I can hear it in your voice."

"RUFF!"

"And your dog sounds like a terrier!"

"HE IS!"

"RUFF!"

"You are clever," said Dilly.

"It is my senses, child. What I lack in one I more than make up for in another! Welsh?"

"YES!"

"South Wales?"

"YES! Gosh, you really are clever! Is Frau Fröhlich in the library?" asked Dilly.

"I didn't see her."

"No. I guess not. Oh! I'm so, so sorry. Please forgive me."

Magnus Magnus smiled. "Forgiven! It happens all the time!"

"What were you doing in the library?"

"I had just performed a piano recital in the ballroom and was retiring to my cabin when I heard noises from inside."

"What noises?"

"A moan and a miaow. Must have been her and her black cat. I opened the door and called out, but there was silence. A deathly silence."

"I must go and check," said Dilly.

"I pray there hasn't been an accident, but this storm has been punishing. Perhaps some books were flung off the shelves?"

Right on cue, another huge wave struck the ship.

SPLOOSH!

They were thrown off balance.

"Are you all right, Mr Magnus Magnus? This storm is a beast!"

"I am fine," he replied. "I know this ship perfectly well by now!" With that, he hurried off along the swaying gangway.

Dilly and Watson rushed away in the opposite direction. When Dilly opened the library door, a macabre sight greeted them.

The books in the library were now in a huge pile in the centre of the room. And sticking out from under the pile was Fröhlich's limp hand.

"FRAU FRÖHLICH!" cried Dilly.

She and Watson clambered over the mountain of books to reach her. Together, they dug her out.

But it was too late.

Fröhlich was dead.

CRUSHED TO DEATH BY MURDER-MYSTERY BOOKS!

In her hand was the monogrammed cufflink.

As Dilly took it, Watson alerted her to a little black paw poking out from under the pile.

"WOOF!"

"Who would kill a cat?" asked Dilly, incredulous.

Watson shrugged his shoulders. He could certainly imagine a scenario where he might.

"We must find the captain at once! Raise the alarm!"

But, as she and Watson scrambled over the books back to the door, it swung open.

Standing in the doorway was the captain, with the maître d', Gladys and Fox. A throng of crew and passengers gathered behind them.

"FRÖHLICH IS DEAD!" exclaimed Dilly.

The captain clambered over the books to reach her and checked her pulse. After a few moments, he bowed his head.

There were shouts from the crowd.

"THAT GIRL MUST BE THE MURDERER!"

"ARREST HER!"

"Before she kills again!"

"LOCK HER UP!"

"The killer has been unmasked!"

"I knew it would be someone Welsh!"

"I KNEW YOU WERE WICKED, DILLY! BUT *MURDER*!" cried Gladys.

"I didn't kill Fröhlich or her cat. Or anyone!"

The mob did not believe her.

"HEARTLESS FIEND!"

"With a face of pure evil!"

"That dog is her accomplice!"

"Force them both to walk the plank!"

"An eye for a tooth!"

"DROWN THE PAIR OF THEM, I SAY!"

"Drowning's too good for them!"

"Feed them to the sharks!"

"SILENCE!" ordered the captain, and there was silence. "NO ONE WILL BE WALKING THE PLANK ON MY WATCH."

"Spoilsport!"

"Fun sponge!"

"Party pooper!"

"I SAID 'SILENCE'!" barked the captain. "I am the captain of this ship! And while we are at sea I am the law!"

Fox put his hand up. The captain nodded to him to speak.

"Thank you, Captain. Please, let me make a heartfelt plea on behalf of Dilly. In the short time I have known her, I promise you I have found her to be a kind girl, a gentle soul with a heart of GOLD. I don't believe for one moment Dilly has anything to do with these murders. She wouldn't harm a flea."

"I, too, am sure of it," replied the captain. "But I think it is best for everyone, not least for her own protection, that for the rest of the journey Miss Dilys be kept under lock and key."

"YES!" exclaimed Gladys.

CHAPTER TWENTY-THREE

DOWN IN THE DEPTHS

In the depths of **THE MASQUERADE** was the engine room. Here, a mountain of coal burned day and night to power the ship across the ocean. There was a deafening drone from the machinery. Huge wheels turned. Men in boiler suits, their hands and faces blackened with soot, hurried around with trucks of coal, keeping this beast fed.

The engine room had a small cell in it. It had a bed, a blanket, a bucket and not much else. It was there in the event that a passenger or crew member needed to be locked up.

A stowaway.

A thief.

The captain had spent a lifetime on the ocean, and a quarter of a century at the helm of **THE MASQUERADE**, but had seen the cell used only a handful of times.

And he had never needed to put a child in there. Or a

dog. His stiff upper lip was trembling as he locked Dilly in. It caused as much sorrow to him as it did to her.

CLICK!

"Captain! Please!" pleaded Dilly. "You know I'm innocent!"

"I am sure, Miss Dilys. I can't bear doing this to you. But it will just be for a couple of nights, until we reach Southampton. I promise. And with that mob after you, and the murderer on the loose, I am sad to say this is the safest place for you."

"Yes, but I am the only detective left standing."

"That's what I'm afraid of. You could be next."

"I don't care about being safe! I need to solve these murders!"

"Miss Dilys, please listen! I can't let you put yourself in any more danger. It's very late. Please try to sleep. I will be back first thing in the morning with a banana milkshake for you, and a sausage for Watson."

"RUFF!"

"This is the safest place on the ship. I promise." The captain turned his head as tears rolled down his cheeks. "I will be back before you know it," he spluttered, before walking away.

Dilly clung to the bars in the window, and cried,

"CAPTAIN!"

But he didn't look back. Or, rather, couldn't.

Being imprisoned was a billion times worse than being grounded. This was the grounding to end all groundings.

Dilly felt helpless. And alone. She couldn't sleep a wink. So she spent all night trying to crack the case.

How could Magnus Magnus know Frau Fröhlich's cat was black?

Was it significant that his name began with M?

Another M!

Just like Morosov.

There was an **M** engraved on the cufflink.

Was one of them the murderer?

Then there was the blind composer himself. **THE MASQUERADE** had been at sea for nearly a week now, yet Dilly had never spotted him on the ship before. And she would remember a blind man with a white stick. Was he, like the brigadier and Morosov and the Black Widow, nowhere to be found in the ship's passenger list? She cast her mind back to it but couldn't remember whether there had been a *Magnus* there.

Did these four know each other?

Were they working together as a pack  of cold-hearted killers?

Dilly had to do some more detective work. She found her paperclip and squeezed her arm through the bars. But, as hard as she tried, she couldn't reach the lock.

"BLAST!"

Dilly lay down on the mattress. Watson leaped up on to it to snuggle next to her.

Then a shadow flickered across the hatch.

"Captain?" she called out.

"No!" said the man, chortling to himself. "But I

might be the captain one day!" he added, in a Scottish accent. "If I work very, very, very, very, very hard! Ha! Ha!"

He came closer. He was covered in soot and had the wildest ginger hair Dilly had ever seen. A wiry bush circled a spot of baldness on the top of his head. He had mutton chops – long, thick sideburns connected to a moustache without the beard on the chin. As if this wasn't enough, more hair sprouted from his ears and nose. His eyes were deep brown. He was wearing a filthy boiler suit, a sweaty neckerchief and stomping great boots.

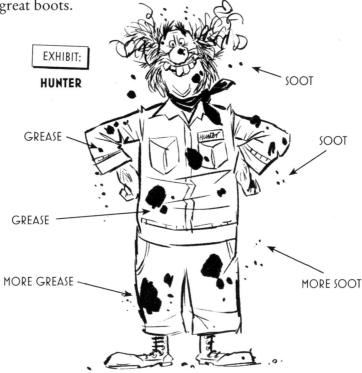

EXHIBIT:
HUNTER

SOOT

GREASE

SOOT

GREASE

MORE GREASE

MORE SOOT

"Who are you?" asked Dilly.

"Hunter!" he replied proudly.

"A hunter?"

"No. Hunter is my name. I'm from Scotland."

"I had deduced that."

"Aye! Canny lass! I work down here in the engine room."

"I'm a detective. I had deduced that too."

"But I bet ye cannae guess my name!"

"Hunter?"

He was astonished. "How did ye know?"

"Lucky guess, I suppose."

"I brought ye some scran," said Hunter.

"What?"

"Food! Us greasers don't get much. We're the lowest of the low. But ye can have me tattie!"

With that, he rummaged deep into his pocket and pulled out a soggy boiled potato.

"Thank you!"

"RUFF!"

"Is that ye wee dog?"

"Yes."

Hunter pushed the boiled potato through the bars,

and it became mashed potato.

Still, any food was welcome right now.

"Thank you! Thank you! Thank you!" she mumbled, her mouth full of food. Watson gobbled up his share from Dilly's cupped hand.

"Why are you being so kind to me?" she asked.

"Ye cannae lock up a wee bairn!"

"Or a dog."

"Right!" he agreed.

"And we are both innocent!"

"Course ye are! These murders have been shocking! And if ye are a detective ye should be up there solving the crime!"

"That's what I told the captain!" cried Dilly.

"So…"

"So?"

"I brought ye this!" he said, dangling a key.

Dilly smiled.

SHE WAS BACK IN THE GAME!

CHAPTER TWENTY-FOUR

DISGUISE

But what a dangerous game this was.

Dilly was now the NUMBER-ONE SUSPECT!

IN NOT ONE, BUT FOUR MURDERS!

FOUR AND A HALF, IF YOU INCLUDED THE CAT!

"Hey, lassie!" said Hunter as she and Watson were scurrying across the engine room.

"Yes?"

"Ye cannae run around like that!"

"Like what?"

"As ye. If the cage is found bare, ye will have the whole ship looking for ye!"

"Of course."

"Ye need to disguise yerself!"

"Good plan! Thanks, Hunter! You're the best!"

Just then a shadow loomed across the wall. Perhaps

one of Hunter's fellow greasers.

"GO! GO! GO!" he said.

Dilly smiled, sneaked behind a boiler and then darted up the spiral staircase.

Three levels up was a vast laundry room. A hundred uniforms were hanging out to dry. A waiter's outfit seemed like the most sensible choice. If she strutted around THE MASQUERADE in the captain's uniform, people might get suspicious.

Dilly found the smallest one, slipped it on and dashed out with Watson trailing behind. As much as she loved him, the dog was going to give the game away, so their next stop was the kitchen.

There, Dilly found a cloche, one of those silver domes that cover plates of food for posh people. She hid a reluctant Watson under it and carried him off as if he were someone's dinner. Which he would rather not be.

"RUFF!"

Dilly caught sight of her reflection in a window. The outfit was perfect, the cloche a masterstroke, but Dilly still looked like Dilly. She needed to disguise her face.

She wet her hair in a sink and parted it, so it looked

more like a man's. Then, after cuddling him and apologising in advance, she yanked some fur from Watson...

"YOUCH!"

... and stuck it to her upper lip with some grease.

HEY PRESTO! She had a moustache!

EXHIBIT:

BEFORE

AFTER

It was now dawn. As soon as Dilly reached the swaying deck, she heard a shout.

"YOU!"

It was the maître d'.

Dilly didn't dare stop and turn round. Instead, she continued striding off with purpose. After all, a passenger might have ordered a terrier for breakfast.

"I SAID 'YOU', WAITER! STOP!"

Now the few passengers who were out for a morning stroll were staring at her. It would have been suspicious to keep going. So she turned round slowly.

"Me?" asked Dilly, affecting her best deep voice.

"YES!" he thundered. "And, as well you know, you call the maître d' 'sir'!"

"Yes, sir. Sorry, sir."

The maître d' strode up to Dilly.

"You look a disgrace!" he barked, flicking Dilly's bow tie.

"Sorry, sir!"

"Who are you? I don't recognise you!"

Dilly had to think fast. "I'm new."

"New?"

"Just joined the ship today."

"We are a thousand miles from land!"

"I mean last week, just before we left New York."

"What is your *nom*?"

Dilly hesitated. "Sherlock."

"Sherlock?"

"Yes."

"Sherlock what?"

"Sherlock Holmes!"

Dilly was UNDER PRESSURE.

Right now, it was the only name she could conjure.

"Is that supposed to be funny?"

"No."

"That is the name of a world-famous detective!"

"Never heard of him."

The maître d' was confounded.

"So, no one has ever mentioned to you that's an odd name to have?"

"Nope!"

"Where are you going, Sherlock?"

"Just to deliver some breakfast to an elderly

passenger," she said, indicating the cloche.

"What's under there?"

"A lobster," she lied, struggling to hold the weight of her dog.

"A lobster? For *petit déjeuner*?"

"That's what she ordered."

"Let me see!"

"No!"

"*Non?*"

"I would let you, but the lobster is so fresh that it is actually still alive, and really quite nippy!"

"Nippy?"

Dilly did a mime of a lobster attacking with its claws. "It's a big un! It'll have your arm off!"

The maître d' was not so easily fooled. He reached for the cloche…

Dilly froze in fear.

CHAPTER TWENTY-FIVE

A FLYING NUN

Just as the maître d' was about to discover a breakfast terrier, there was a commotion on deck.

"A BOAT!" cried someone, pointing out at sea.

This distracted the maître d'. He rushed over to the side to see. Dilly followed from a safe distance.

"A SPEEDBOAT!"

"IT'S FOLLOWING US!"

"THERE ARE TWO MEN!"

Indeed, there were. Two men Dilly immediately recognised. The detective duo Cyril and Cuthbert! A pair of English upper-class twits who solved crimes together. Cyril was piloting the speedboat as Cuthbert water-skied behind.

SWOOSH!

Both were soaked to the skin from the storm.

"I SAY!" cried Cyril.

"Do you mind awfully if we climb aboard?" asked Cuthbert.

Both were clutching glasses of champagne, half full of sea water.

The two detectives were a couple, and never seen apart.

EXHIBIT: **CYRIL**

EXHIBIT: **CUTHBERT**

STRAW BOATER

PONG OF CHAMPAGNE

PONGIER PONG OF CHAMPAGNE

FLOPPY DOPPY WOPPY HAIR

PENCIL MOUSTACHE

SILK CRAVAT

CLUB TIE

STRIPY BLAZER

TENNIS RACQUET

TEDDY BEAR (DRESSED IDENTICALLY)

CREAM SLACKS

SILK DRESSING GOWN

VELVET MONOGRAMMED SLIPPERS

SILK PYJAMA

PLIMSOLLS

Together, Cyril and Cuthbert had solved many murder mysteries in the great country houses of England. They only solved the murders of other upper-class twits just like them. That way you could stay over and enjoy a free holiday, feasting on pheasant, taking in a game of croquet on the lawn and raiding the wine cellar.

Solving a murder came second to all the fun.

Their celebrated cases included:

- **THE POISONED PAVLOVA**
- **THE SCOUNDREL IN THE SCULLERY**
- **THE BUTLER DID IT**
- **NOT IN FRONT OF MOTHER**
- **DEATH BY CUCUMBER SANDWICHES**
- **BLOOD ON THE CROQUET MALLET**
- **THE EXPLODING BILLIARD BALL**
- **NANNY'S REVENGE**
- **THE ROTTER IN THE ROLLS**
- **MY PAPA'S A DUKE SO WOULD YOU MIND AWFULLY LETTING ME ORF?**

The moment Cyril and Cuthbert boarded **THE MASQUERADE**, they announced, "We are here to enjoy a free cruise!" and, "Quaff the ship dry of champers!"

The pair clinked their glasses, and in unison cried,
"BOTTOMS UP!"

"Oh! And solve a pesky little murder or two."

"Only if there's time. I do want to enjoy some spa treatments!"

"Couple's massage! WAITER!"

Dilly looked round, remembering that she was supposed to be one.

"Me?" she asked.

"YES! YOU, BOY! FETCH YOUR FINEST BOTTLE OF CHAMPERS!"

"Right away, sir!"

Then she realised she had no clue where the wine cellar was. Something a waiter would one hundred per cent know. She took a chance by hurrying to the bow of the ship.

"WRONG WAY!" shouted the maître d', stepping into Dilly's path.

"Sorry?"

"The *vin* cellar is this way."

"Of course! Silly me!"

"I will take the lobster!" declared the maître d', reaching out his hand.

"WHERE IS OUR CHAMPERS?" cried Cyril.

"Coming right up, gentlemen!" replied Dilly, scurrying away from the maître d'.

But, just as she was about to race down the staircase, she spied what looked like a giant seagull swooping over the ship.

"CHAMPAGNE IS THE DEVIL'S WORK!" came a voice from the clouds.

IT WAS A NUN!

A FLYING NUN!

CHAPTER TWENTY-SIX

BIKE-O-PLANE

It was not just any nun, but Sister Ruth, the celebrated nun **detective**! She was riding a bicycle-plane of her own invention, battling against the storm.

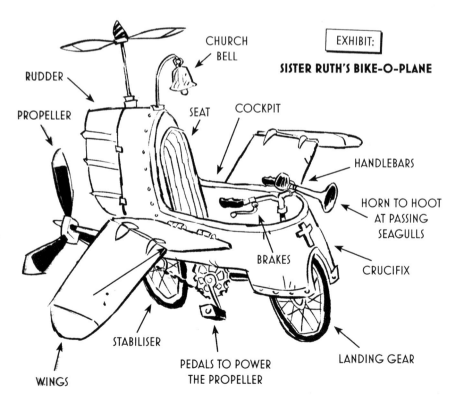

CHURCH BELL

EXHIBIT:

SISTER RUTH'S BIKE-O-PLANE

RUDDER

PROPELLER

SEAT

COCKPIT

HANDLEBARS

HORN TO HOOT AT PASSING SEAGULLS

BRAKES

CRUCIFIX

STABILISER

LANDING GEAR

WINGS

PEDALS TO POWER THE PROPELLER

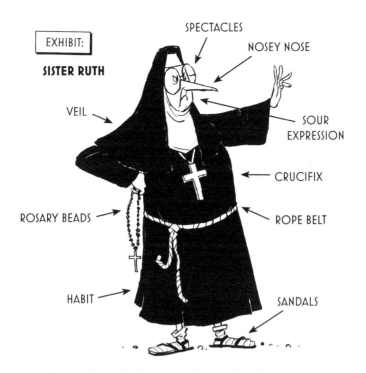

EXHIBIT:

SISTER RUTH

SPECTACLES

NOSEY NOSE

VEIL

SOUR EXPRESSION

CRUCIFIX

ROSARY BEADS

ROPE BELT

HABIT

SANDALS

Dilly had read all the nun's casebooks:

- **THE BODY IN THE ORGAN**
- **THE VOW OF DOOM**
- **THE CURSED CONVENT**
- **ORDER TO MURDER**
- **REVENGE OF THE RENOUNCED WORLDLY GOODS**
- **ABBESS AT THE ABYSS**
- **THE POISONED PRAYER BOOK**
- **NIGHTMARE AT THE NUNNERY**
- **THE MURDEROUS MONK**
- **A VERY BAD HABIT**

As soon as the wheels of her Bike-o-Plane touched the deck, she cried, "CAPTAIN! CAPTAIN!"

"Welcome aboard, Sister Ruth," he said as he hurried over to her.

Cuthbert and Cyril seethed.

"Not that ghastly nun again!"

"Always ruins it for us!"

"You don't need to tell me, dear!"

"Don't snap at me, dear!"

"I am not snapping, dear!"

Meanwhile, the captain offered up his arm to assist Sister Ruth.

"I am perfectly capable, Captain," she scolded. "I received the telegram you sent to the Vatican! Two detectives dead! And, even worse, a dead cat! And I

believe you have a prime suspect. A child of the girl variety?"

"Yes, but I don't think for a moment she could have done it."

"I will be the judge of that! There are many wicked children in the world. Take me to her at once!"

From her hiding place behind a funnel, panic flashed across Dilly's face. If they found out she had escaped, she would be in deep, deep doo-doo!

Cuthbert and Cyril scampered over to the nun.

"Excuse me, Sister!" began Cyril. "We were here first!"

"The suspect is ours to question!" added Cuthbert.

"Just as soon as we've had our champers!" said Cyril.

"Rather!" agreed Cuthbert.

"Captain! Do not let this pair of clowns quaff any more champagne!" thundered Sister Ruth.

"We'll quaff as much as we like!"

"We're a pair of quaffers!"

"NO, YOU WILL NOT! Drinking alcohol is a vice! A terrible vice! That is why I only drink whiskey!"

With that, she took a silver hip flask out from under her habit and downed the lot in one.

"AAH! That's better!" she said.

"Sister Ruth, Cuthbert and I demand you leave this ship at once!"

"NEVER!" she said, lighting a thick cigar. She purposefully blew the smoke into Cyril's face. He put on a big performance of coughing and spluttering.

Dilly stifled a giggle.

"Cuthbert! That dastardly nun just blew smoke in my face!"

"How dare you do that to my Cyril!"

TORPEDC

"Oh! I do dare! I do!" replied Sister Ruth, now blowing thick black smoke into Cuthbert's face.

"EURGH!"

"Do that to my Cuthbert again, and I'll scream and scream and scream until I'm sick!" cried Cyril.

Sister Ruth grinned and took a deep drag on her cigar. But, just before she could goad anyone further, the captain interrupted.

"PLEASE! I have four dead bodies on this ship!"

"And a dead cat!" added Sister Ruth.

"And a dead cat! Four and a half dead bodies! And I don't need another! So, please, please, please stop bickering!"

"HEAR, HEAR, CAPTAIN!" came a voice from the ocean.

Passengers and crew looked over to see that a submarine had emerged from the waves.

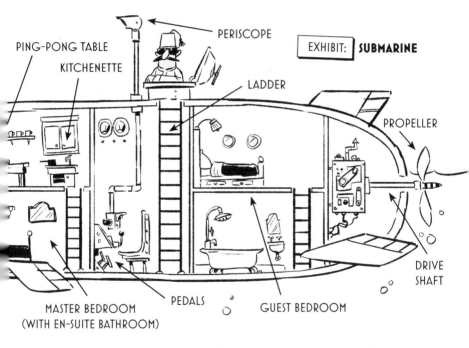

PERISCOPE

PING-PONG TABLE

KITCHENETTE

EXHIBIT: **SUBMARINE**

LADDER

PROPELLER

DRIVE SHAFT

MASTER BEDROOM
(WITH EN-SUITE BATHROOM)

PEDALS

GUEST BEDROOM

A distinguished-looking gentleman had popped his head out of the hatch. It was the unmistakable figure of Shariff, the Egyptian master detective.

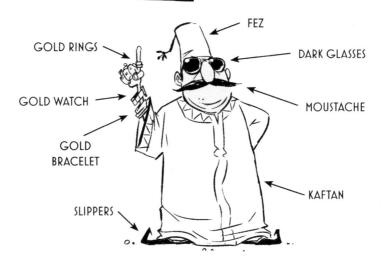

FEZ

GOLD RINGS

DARK GLASSES

GOLD WATCH

MOUSTACHE

GOLD BRACELET

KAFTAN

SLIPPERS

Dilly had, of course, read all of Shariff's casebooks too:

- **THE BODY IN THE CARPET**
- **THE MINT–TEA MURDERS**
- **THE CURSE OF THE MUMMIFIED CAT**
- **DESSERT IN THE DESERT**
- **DESERT IN THE DESSERT**
- **THE VERY RED SEA**
- **THE DEATH MASK OF DEATH**
- **THE RIDDLE OF THE SLIPPER PRINT ON THE BOTTOM**
- **THE PYRAMID SCHEME**
- **CAMEL OF THE BASKERVILLES**

"IT IS I! SHARIFF!" he announced proudly.

He took a drag from his ornate hubbly bubbly pipe, before a huge wave crashed over him.

SPLOOSH!

"I, AND I ALONE, WILL SOLVE THE MURDERS!"

"NOOOOOOOOOOOOOOOO!" cried the other three.

It was an embarrassment of detectives.

By the stroke of midnight, all of them would be dead.

DUM! DUM! DUM!

ACT IV

DEATH BY CHAMPERS

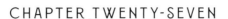

CHAPTER TWENTY-SEVEN

FLATTENED FEZ

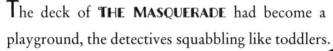

The deck of **THE MASQUERADE** had become a playground, the detectives squabbling like toddlers.

Dilly had to stifle a giggle.

Shariff adopted a mocking tone.

"So this is my competition! A pair of clowns and BATNUN!"

"BATNUN?" exclaimed Sister Ruth. "TAKE THAT BACK!"

"BATNUN! BATNUN! BATNUN!" he chanted.

Cyril and Cuthbert joined in too.

"BATNUN! BATNUN! BATNUN!"

A wicked grin crept across Sister Ruth's face. She twirled her habit as if it were a pair of bat wings.

SWOOSH!

For a moment, the other three could only see black.

It was enough time for her to slip off a sock and sandal.

228

Then she whacked Shariff on the head with it.

THWACK!

His fez was flattened.

He took it off his head and inspected it before putting it back.

"You will pay for this, Batnun!" said Shariff, holding up his hands, ready to do battle.

The nun performed a daring flying kick and foot-slapped him.

He hit the deck.

THUD!

"OOF!"

"YOU BRUTE!" cried Cyril.

"YOU HEARTLESS BRUTE!"

He leaned down to help Shariff up. As he bent over, Batnun spanked him hard on the bottom with her sandal.

"OW!"

He fell on to Shariff.

"GET OFF ME, YOU BUFFOON!"

cried the little man.

"SHE HIT ME ON THE BOTTOM! CUTHBERT! DO SOMETHING!"

Cuthbert brandished his teddy bear. "This is Quentin! And I am not afraid to use him!"

He lunged at her with his teddy, but she whacked it with her sandal.

T H W A C K !
WHIZZ!

The teddy bear flew over everyone's heads and over the side of the ship.

"NOOOOOO!"

Cyril and Shariff scrambled to their feet.

"CAPTAIN!" cried Cuthbert. "Turn this ship around! We must save Quentin from drowning!"

The teddy bear was being tossed on the waves.

"DON'T BE ABSURD!" yelled the captain. "NOW, ALL OF YOU! BEHAVE!"

"*She* started it!" protested Shariff. "Look what she did to my fez!"

Sister Ruth snatched the crumpled hat from him and punched her hand through the top.

THWUP!

Then she plonked it
on his head.

"There you go, Shariff!"

Fuming, he snatched her rosary
beads and stuffed them up her nose.

"EURGH!"

She yanked his fez off and
slapped him on his bald head
with her sandal.

SLAP!
"OUCH!"

Dilly was amazed at how much chaos a nun
could create with just one sandal. She shuddered
to think what she might achieve with two.

Meanwhile, Cyril wielded his tennis racquet, using
his straw boater as a shield.

"Anyone for tennis?"

The nun put her fist straight through his straw
boater…

CRUMP!

...giving it a sunroof.

As Cyril cowered, she snatched his tennis racquet and yanked off one of his plimsolls. Then she hurled the plimsoll in the air and whacked it into the furthest funnel.

THWACK!

"YOU BRUTE! YOU HEARTLESS BRUTE!" cried Cyril.

"STOP THIS NONSENSE NOW!" barked the captain.

"Or what?" demanded Sister Ruth.

The nun was on a roll now. She spun the racquet round as fast as she could while throwing her sandal up in the air, ready to strike again.

"Or I will shut the bar for the rest of the journey!"

In an instant, they all fell silent.

"You are here to catch a killer!"

"Are we?" asked Cuthbert.

"**YES!**" thundered the captain.

"I will take charge!" announced Sister Ruth.

"No! I am the senior detective!" protested Shariff. "I will take charge!"

"Cuthbert and I are by far the poshest, though, so we will take charge!"

"**I AM IN CHARGE!**" said the captain. "Sister Ruth, you may start in the engine room."

"**YES!**" she exclaimed.

"I will accompany you. Miss Dilys is only twelve, and I believe with all my heart that she is innocent."

"We will see."

"Cyril and Cuthbert," continued the captain, "you can search the Maestro's cabin."

"I wonder if there's a bottle or two of champers in there?" said Cyril.

"**Bottoms up!**" added Cuthbert.

"And, Shariff?" said the captain. "Frau Fröhlich was found dead under a pile of books, so you begin in the library."

"YES!" he said, racing off, the top of his fez flapping in the wind.

"Where do you think you are going?" called the captain.

"The library!" replied Shariff, skidding to a halt.

"On my signal and not before! I am not having tears before bedtime. Form a line, please. When I blow my whistle, off you go!"

The four detectives huffed and formed a line.

The captain took his whistle out of his pocket.

Sister Ruth lurched forward.

"WAIT FOR IT!"

Then Cyril and Cuthbert made a false start.

"WAIT!"

Shariff tried to tiptoe off.

"I SAID 'WAIT'!"

Then he stayed dead still.

"Shariff! This isn't a game of Grandma's Footsteps! Back to the line!"

Shariff huffed and took a pace back, as the other three shook their heads and tutted.

"TUT! TUT! TUT!"

All this reminded Dilly of the egg-and-spoon race in her first year at school.

The captain brought his whistle to his lips and…

TOOT!

…they were off!

CHAPTER TWENTY-EIGHT

A GIANT FOOT

Despite her advanced years, Sister Ruth surged ahead of the others. The captain trailed after her.

"WAIT FOR ME!"

But instead of using the stairs the nun straddled the banister and slid down it at lightning speed.

WHOOSH!

As she whizzed past a waiter on the stairs, she whipped the tray from his hand and downed the banana milkshake from it in one go.

"BURP!"

Dilly needed to reach the engine room before Sister Ruth did. If the nun found her missing, she would look as guilty as sin.

So she found **THE MASQUERADE'S** coal chute. Using the tray as a sledge, she and Watson slid down the long, long, long tube.

WHOOSH!

IT WAS THE WORLD'S DEADLIEST
HELTER-SKELTER!

WHOOSH!

The pair landed with a bump on a mountain
of coal.

THWUD!

The coal began to slide beneath them.

SCHWUM!

They tumbled down to the engine-room
floor.

DRUMP!

They dug themselves out of the
coal and Dilly did her best
to pat the dust off as she
raced towards
the cell.

Her little white dog was now a little black dog.

Before they reached the cell, Watson spotted something strange on the floor. It was poking out from behind a piece of heavy machinery.

"WOOF! WOOF! WOOF!" he barked, alerting his mistress.

It looked like a giant foot. A flattened giant foot. No thicker than a pancake, but as wide as a bed. She turned the corner to get a better look.

SHOCK! HORROR!

"ARGH!" screamed Dilly.

It was Sister Ruth! A huge, flat Sister Ruth! The nun had been squished by one of the giant wheels.

Despite Dilly having taught herself first aid, there was nothing she could do for the nun now.

She was dead.

Deader than dead.

Dead dead.

It looked as if it could have been an accident, but Dilly was sure it was no such thing.

THE KILLER HAD STRUCK AGAIN.

She had to warn the other detectives that they were in

MORTAL DANGER!

"Watson! To the Maestro's cabin!" she cried.

"WOOF!"

Moments later, the pair burst into the room.

Dilly called out their names.

"CYRIL! CUTHBERT! ARE YOU HERE?"

But Cuthbert and Cyril were nowhere to be seen.

Then she heard fizzing from the bathroom.

FIZZ!

She opened the bathroom door to investigate: there were magnums of champagne rolling on the floor.

The fizzing was coming from the bath.

FIZZ!

It was full to the brim with a froth on top, like a layer of bubble bath. As she approached, Dilly realised this wasn't water – it had the sweet smell of champagne.

She took a deep breath before sweeping the froth away.

More SHOCK! More HORROR!

The detective couple were drowned in champagne!

"ARGH!" screamed Dilly.

It was a ghoulish scene.

The quaffers had quaffed their last quaff.

Three down. One to go.

"SHARIFF!" cried Dilly.

"RUFF!"

When she and Watson burst into the library, they found the most horrific sight yet.

"ARGH!"

The model of THE MASQUERADE had been removed, and Shariff had been squeezed inside the giant bottle! The cork was in place. He must have run out of air, like a wasp in a jar, or farted and gassed himself.

Now Dilly was the last detective standing. She had to blow her own cover and alert the captain at once. She must be next on THE HIT LIST!

She wriggled out of her waiter's jacket and trousers and hurled them on to the floor. But she forgot to rip off her moustache.

It wasn't until Dilly turned to go that she realised someone was standing at the doorway.

The maître d'.

"FINALLY, YOU HAVE BEEN CAUGHT! *ROUGE*-HANDED!"

CHAPTER TWENTY-NINE

SILENT SCREAM

"I promise on Watson's life that I had nothing to do with these murders!" pleaded Dilly.

"The *mademoiselle* of *déguisement* has struck again!" said the maître d'.

"I am not a *mademoiselle* of *déguisement*!"

"Then why do you have a moustache glued to your face?"

Dilly panicked and felt above her upper lip. It was still there. So she ripped it off…

"YOUCH!"

…before sticking it back on to Watson.

"RUFF!"

"You used the art of *déguisement* to commit the murders!"

"NO!"

"Then why did I just spy you fleeing from the scenes

of the crimes? The nun. The twits. The man in the flippy-flappy fez?"

"Because I was doing my detective work."

"An elaborate ruse!"

"I don't have a motive."

"JEALOUSY!"

"Of whom?"

"Of these genius detectives! No one on this ship will be safe unless you are hurled into the ocean! Now come here!"

As the maître d' lunged at Dilly, Watson launched himself at the man's bottom. The dog opened his mouth wide and took a mighty CHOMP!

CHOMP!

"YOUCH!" yelled the maître d' as he writhed in bum-based agony.

The shout must have alerted passing passengers, because soon an angry mob had gathered at the library door.

"YOUR KILLING SPREE IS OVER!"

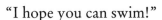

"I hope you can swim!"

"AND THAT MUTT OF YOURS!"

"Because you are both going to be hurled over the side!"

"You can't escape this time!"

The maître d' staggered to his feet. "*REGARDEZ* WHAT THE MURDERER'S *CHIEN* DID TO MY *DERRIÈRE*!" he cried, bending over to show the hole in his trousers and the bite mark on his cheek.

"EURGH!"

"Put it away!"

"That's going to put me right off my dinner!"

"GRAB HER!" shouted someone.

The mob pushed past the captain and formed a circle round Dilly.

"GRRR!" growled Watson, trying to scare them off, but the circle got smaller and smaller and smaller.

Dilly, however, wasn't giving up without a fight! There was only one thing between her and them.

THE MODEL OF THE MASQUERADE!

She lifted it up. It was heavy, but she spun it round as if it were a flaming torch.

"BACK OFF!"

But they wouldn't. Arms stretched out to grab her.
Then…

THWUP!

The ship lurched as another huge wave struck.

CRASH!

The storm was worsening by the minute.

Books were hurled off the shelves. They bonked the

heads of the mob…

BOOF! BOOF! BOOF!

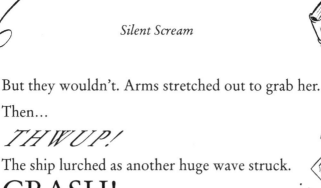

…knocking them to the floor.

DOOF! DOOF! DOOF!

As the ship swayed from side to side, everyone had to hold on to the nailed-down furniture to avoid being tossed across the room.

However, with her arms full of dog and model ship, Dilly stumbled backwards. The pointy end of the model struck a porthole, smashing it.

CRACK!

Ice-cold water gushed in, flooding the library and sweeping everyone off their feet.

"ARGH!"
"HELP!
"I HAVEN'T GOT MY TRUNKS ON!"
Dilly dropped Watson.

SPLOSH!

Having little legs, he had to doggy-paddle to keep his head above the water.

"RUFF!"

Dilly dropped the model ship too.

SPLOOSH!

It floated, which gave Dilly a magnificent idea.

PING!

"Watson! Jump on! We're going surfing!"

CHAPTER THIRTY

UPSIDE DOWN

That's what they did. As the library filled with water, books floating on the surface, DILLY AND WATSON SURFED OUT OF THE ROOM ON THE GIANT MODEL OF THE MASQUERADE!

SWOOSH!

Everyone had to SWIM out of the way, as the ship surfed a wave.

SPLASH! SPLOSH! SPLUSH!

"NOOOO!"

"STOP THEM!"

"HAS ANYONE SEEN MY SHOE?"

As water flooded out into the gangway, our heroes were carried off.

Passengers and crew leaped aside as they surfed past them.

"OOH!"

"AH!"

"PLEASE MIND WHERE YOU ARE SURFING!"

"IS BINGO ON AGAIN TODAY?"

Dilly grinned. This was thrilling. But soon the flood became a trickle and the model ship grounded.

SCRUNCH!

The pair wobbled, before leaping off.

Both soaking wet, they left footprints and pawprints in their wake.

The only person Dilly could turn to now was Fox, so she bolted to his cabin.

Right now, they needed his help more than ever. He was clever. He was kind. He knew she was innocent. And he would know what to do.

So, reeling with the storm, she pounded on his door.

KNOCK! KNOCK! KNOCK!

"FOX? FOX?"

But there was no answer!

"No!" cried Dilly in frustration.

She and Watson could hear the angry mob drawing near.

Hands trembling, Dilly picked the lock with her paperclip.

CLICK!

"BINGO!"

She opened the door and the pair fell into the cabin.

They stayed still on the floor, not daring to breathe, as the mob passed.

"WHERE IS SHE?"

"LET'S BREAK DOWN THE DOOR TO HER CABIN!"

"I STILL CAN'T FIND MY SHOE!"

Next there was the sound of thuds.

THUD! THUD! THUD!

After a few goes, the door must have swung open as the maître d' cried, "The *petite* demon isn't here! Let's all spread out and search the entire ship! Starting with all *les cabines*!"

"WE MIGHT EVEN FIND MY SHOE!"

Still lying on the floor, Dilly spotted a mark on the huge luggage trunk that she hadn't noticed before – hardly surprising as it was faded, just a slight discoloration on the leather. She wriggled closer to get a better look.

It seemed to be a letter.

Yes…

It was.

It was a "W".

A metal letter W must have been removed from the trunk, leaving the faintest imprint behind.

"Who is W?" she asked herself.

Then she paused.

Wait.

"THE CUFFLINK!" exclaimed Dilly, taking it out of her pocket. "What if it isn't an M engraved on it? What if it's a W?"

Dilly stared at the trunk. All this time she'd been looking for an M.

Morosov. Magnus.

But what if she'd had it all upside down?

What if she should have been looking for a W all along?

She turned the cufflink over.

M became W.

Fingers trembling, she picked the lock of Fox's trunk.

Then she opened it, her tummy churning.

The trunk was full of clothes.

Or rather costumes.

A brigadier's uniform.

The long tunic that the Russian novelist Morosov wore.

A widow's weeds, complete with black patent-leather heeled shoes and a veil.

A greasy boiler suit with the name "HUNTER" sewn on to it.

A white stick that belonged to the blind composer, Magnus Magnus.

But what really stunned her was the make-up, fake noses, wigs and teeth. Even false ears!

Dilly was reeling with shock.

All the strange people she'd encountered – even the Scottish boiler worker who'd helped her escape the cell, and encouraged her to disguise herself...

All of them... were Lord Fox.

CHAPTER THIRTY-ONE

THE FINAL PIECE
OF THE PUZZLE

Dazed, Dilly continued to search the trunk. In addition to the disguises Lord Fox had used to create the mysterious passengers, there were wigs, fake beards and moustaches, a bald cap, even contact lenses to change his eye colour. Plus boxes and boxes of make-up.

There was a jumble of hairclips, all bent and twisted, that he must have used to pick locks, a bottle of poison, some sticks of dynamite and a deadly scorpion in a jar!

Dilly's face went white.

With all these items removed, she noticed something else: there was an odd gap at the wooden base of the trunk. Feeling around it, she found that she could prise up the edges.

Lifting it, she found a hidden compartment. And, when she looked inside, she found the final piece of the puzzle.

There was a cache of playbills from Broadway shows. Dilly flicked through the pages of these theatre programmes and found pictures of an actor who looked like Fox named Max Wolf.

W.

W for **Wolf.**

There were pictures of him in numerous guises from plays he had performed in.

A MEDIEVAL KING

A VAMPIRE

A JUDGE

A PIRATE

A POLICEMAN

A ROMAN EMPEROR

A KNIGHT

A BUTLER

A FLYING ACE

A WIZENED OLD WITCH

THIS MAN WAS A MASTER OF DISGUISE!

Not only were all the people Dilly had met while doing her detective work merely this actor's characters…

LORD FOX WAS JUST A CHARACTER TOO!

Nor was that all. Lifting everything out, Dilly found a scrapbook at the very bottom of the trunk. This was the most ghoulish discovery of all. Pasted on the pages were newspaper clippings.

The headlines read:

DASTARDLY VILLAIN ON THE LOOSE!

LADY KILLER STRIKES AGAIN!

BODY FOUND IN HUDSON RIVER!

ANOTHER NIGHT, ANOTHER MURDER!

MAESTRO FAILS TO CRACK MULTIPLE MURDER CASE!

KILLER'S PRISON BREAKOUT!

LADY KILLER ON THE RUN!

MURDERER SPOTTED IN MONTE CARLO CASINO!

WIDOW BITTEN BY BLACK WIDOW SPIDER!

IS THIS THE FACE OF THE MOST WANTED MAN IN THE WORLD?

Only someone unspeakably evil would keep these mementos of his crimes.

Wolf used his numerous guises to meet rich single ladies, murder them and inherit all their money.

"Watson! Auntie Gladys is his next victim!"

Their wedding was moments away!

Just as the pair turned to leave, they heard the door-handle rattle.

Dilly and Watson went to hide in the wardrobe, but as they opened the door – shock, horror – a body fell out!

Dilly let out a SILENT SCREAM!

The body fell on top of her.

But wait.

It was light.

This wasn't a dead body. It was a mannequin, a shop-window dummy, dressed as a nurse. The widow's nurse! She hadn't been pushing the bathchair after all! The dummy had been riding on the back of it!

Wolf was clever. Devilishly clever.

Dilly bundled the mannequin back into the wardrobe, and leaped in, closing the door behind them.

At that exact moment, the cabin door swung open. From inside the wardrobe the pair heard footsteps, and a man muttering to himself in an American accent. This must be Wolf's real voice.

"Where *is* that darned cufflink?"

The cufflink he had lost in the Maestro's cabin!

From inside the wardrobe, Dilly and Watson could hear this monster pacing around the cabin. They tried their best not to breathe. He would kill them both without a care.

Watson must have been hungry; he never did get that sausage. His tummy gurgled.

SQUIRB!

The sound of the steps stopped.

Wolf paced over to the wardrobe.

He was so close Dilly could hear him breathing.

CLICK!

He put his hand on the handle.

THEY WERE DONE FOR!

But just then there was the sound of banging.

KNOCK! KNOCK! KNOCK!

"AH! MY DARLING GLADYS!" Now his voice was back to the posh English one he had been faking all this time.

"Come on, my handsome! You're gonna be late for your own wedding!"

"I am coming, my one true love!"

Just as Dilly opened the wardrobe to warn her aunt, the cabin door slammed shut.

SHUNT!

Dilly raced to the door, but when she opened it Auntie Gladys was gone.

"WATSON! WE MUST STOP THIS WEDDING!"

"RUFF!"

ACT V

DEATH BY
MARRIAGE

CHAPTER THIRTY-TWO

WOO, MARRY, MURDER

As Dilly dashed to the ballroom, she began piecing together the timeline of the murders.

When confronting Wolf, she needed to be one hundred per cent sure of every tiny detail. After all, grown-ups had a nasty habit of not believing children.

Dilly felt wretched. Lord Fox, the only person who had ever been kind to her, was really a merciless murderer. But there was no time for feeling sad: she was a detective.

And, as a detective, she had two jobs: unmask Wolf, and save her aunt.

The captain must have conducted the wedding service super-fast, because when Dilly and Watson burst into the ballroom, he announced…

"I now pronounce you man and wife. You may kiss the bride!"

The captain was standing on a small stage with Wolf and Gladys. There was a jazz band to one side, poised to play for the first dance. An assortment of passengers and crew were the wedding guests, all looking queasy as the ship battled through the storm.

The very-newlyweds kissed, and Gladys handed her new husband a glass of champagne, holding one back for herself.

"STOP THIS WEDDING!" cried Dilly.

All eyes turned to the door, where the little drowned rat of a girl and her dog were standing.

"ARREST HER!" shouted someone.

"SHE'S THE KILLER!" cried another.

"I've found my shoe! Oh, no, it's somebody else's! SORRY!" said a third.

"LET ME SPEAK!" demanded Dilly. "THIS MAN IS THE MURDERER!"

She pointed at Wolf.

There was silence for a moment, before he burst out laughing.

"Ha! Ha! Ha!"

Gladys and all the guests joined in too.

"HA! HA! HA!"

Only the captain remained stony-faced.

"Is this some kind of joke?" asked Wolf.

"This is no joke."

The man's eyes narrowed. "You are blaming me for your own dastardly crimes?"

"Let's listen to what Miss Dilys has to say," said the captain.

"NO! NO! NO!" came shouts from the guests.

"Grab her!"

"Take her up to the deck!"

"And fling her overboard!"

"We can watch her drown!"

"As long as it's quick, as I am having a pedicure at six!"

"SILENCE!" thundered the captain. And there was silence. "Miss Dilys, please speak."

Wolf shifted on his feet uneasily. Dilly could tell he was rattled. She took a deep breath and began. She would have to think clearly and speak calmly if she were to persuade everyone that this charming man was a cold-hearted killer.

"Lord Fox is not this man's name," she said. "He is not an English aristocrat – he is an American actor named Max Wolf."

"PREPOSTEROUS!" he scoffed.

"BE QUIET," barked the captain.

"But you can't believe—" spluttered Wolf.

"THAT'S AN ORDER!" bellowed the captain.

"Thank you, Captain," Dilly replied. "Wolf has assumed numerous guises over the years, but his plan was always the same. Find a filthy-rich single lady, woo her, marry her and then murder her."

Gladys looked at her new husband, shocked. "How do you know all this?" she asked Dilly.

"You forget I am a detective!"

"Well, you play at being one," replied Gladys.

"This was not playing. This case was real. Frighteningly so. Now, this is the stage in any murder mystery when the detective **explains** how the murders were committed," continued Dilly.

"OOOH!" went the guests.

"I like this bit."

"I hope I can follow it."

"Sorry, young lady, do you mind holding on a moment before you begin? I want to pop to the little boys' room first as I need a pee-pee."

"NO! HOLD IT IN!" bellowed the captain. He could be very commanding when he wanted to be.

"I FINALLY FOUND MY SHOE! IT WAS ON MY FOOT THE WHOLE TIME!" piped up someone.

"BE QUIET, YOU FOOL!" shouted the captain.

A deathly hush descended on the ballroom.

"Thank you!" said Dilly. "Now let me begin…"

CHAPTER THIRTY-THREE

THE DENOUEMENT

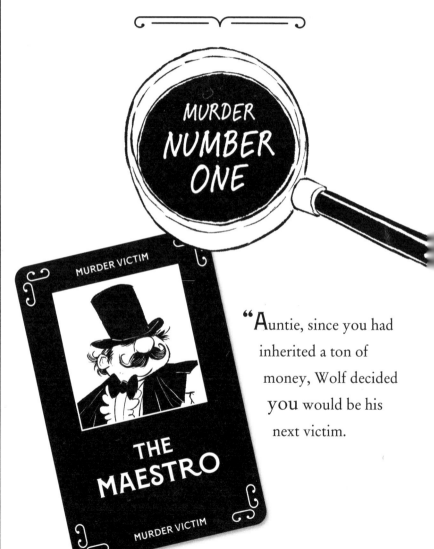

MURDER
NUMBER
ONE

MURDER VICTIM

THE
MAESTRO

MURDER VICTIM

"Auntie, since you had inherited a ton of money, Wolf decided **you** would be his next victim.

This round trip to New York was all part of his wicked plan to make you fall in love with him; make you accept his proposal of marriage. This was thwarted when an unexpected passenger boarded THE MASQUERADE.

The Maestro!

The great detective had been on the trail of the infamous Lady Killer for many years, but Wolf had always eluded him. That was until the Maestro thought he recognised him when taking his morning stroll on the deck.

Wolf must have known he was in grave danger. So, at dinner, he absented himself from the captain's table to fetch your missing earring from your cabin. Really, he must have slyly slipped it off your ear when he caressed your cheek. Then hidden it in his pocket. Remember, you were sure you had put both earrings on.

His plan was to murder the Maestro before the great detective realised he was sitting at the same table as a notorious murderer.

Being an actor, Wolf was able to perform a quick change from his white tie and tails into the brigadier's uniform and make-up.

DISGUISE

THE
BRIGADIER

DISGUISE

Then he went to the Maestro's cabin to murder him. But he was too late. The Maestro had just left for dinner.

Wolf's cufflink fell off in the cabin.

It must be hard to fix it in place when you have one arm tied behind your back. I will return to this, as it's a crucial detail.

Then, he went to the kitchen, pretending to be the drunk old military man, brandy in hand. There he found the Maestro inspecting the dessert.

Wolf drowned him in the giant blancmange!

MURDER WEAPON

A BLANCMANGE

MURDER WEAPON

MURDER
NUMBER
TWO

MURDER VICTIM

THE
CHEF

MURDER VICTIM

Chef must have disturbed Wolf in the act of drowning the Maestro, because he was whacked over the head with his own whisk. I found specks of blood on it.

Then Wolf carried the unconscious chef to the ice room, stripped him down to his undercrackers and left him to freeze to death in there. Following this, he carried Chef's uniform to the stern of the ship, so he could fake the man's death.

MURDER WEAPON

THE ICE ROOM

MURDER WEAPON

Next, Wolf quickly changed back into his Lord Fox costume, and took his seat at the captain's table. He acted shocked when the Maestro was found dead in the blancmange.

A little later, in the early hours of the morning, Watson and I sneaked out of our cabin to investigate.

Noticing the peculiar pattern of footprints on the kitchen floor, I sketched them in my notebook. Later, I realised there weren't two pairs of feet, there were three! So, if the Maestro was one, and Chef the other, who did the third pair belong to?

Chef's hat had fallen off in the struggle. Watson found it under a kitchen counter. Then he followed Chef's scent to the stern of the ship.

SNIFF SNIFF

There, in the fog, we met a peculiar little fellow who claimed to be a famous Russian novelist named Morosov. Again, although I didn't realise it at the time, this was in fact another of Wolf's characters.

DISGUISE

MOROSOV

DISGUISE

He wore a long tunic and must have been on his knees to make himself look so short.

Wolf, disguised as Morosov, said he had seen Chef leap off the ship. Case closed! Chef murdered the Maestro, and then drowned at sea!

But the case wasn't closed, because Watson sniffed out a trail of brandy spots. They began at the stern, which placed the brigadier at the scene too.

The captain found us there and ordered us back to our cabin. But we are the world's number-one little-girl-and-little-dog detective duo, so we slipped off to investigate.

The trail of brandy spots led us all the way to the ice room.

There, I made a horrifying discovery: the dead body of Chef encased in a block of ice!

This was now the early hours of the morning. Wolf sneaked out of his cabin to retrace his steps, most likely to cover up any clues he had left behind.

Following me to the ice room, he slammed and locked the door, leaving me to freeze to death.

It was only thanks to Watson dragging the captain down there by his trouser leg that I am still alive to tell the tale!

MURDER NUMBER THREE

MURDER VICTIM

THE PROFESSOR

MURDER VICTIM

I thought there might be a clue to the identity of Maestro's murderer in his cabin, so Watson and I stole in, and read the master detective's final diary entry.

The Maestro had written that he had recognised a face from his past on the ship.

Just as I had finished reading, Wolf broke in, disguised as the Black Widow. She was in a bath chair, being pushed by a nurse. But there was no nurse! It was a dummy all along! Wolf read the diary, and then tore out the final page and burned it.

DISGUISE

THE BLACK WIDOW

DISGUISE

However, when hiding under the bed, I found a cufflink. It had what I thought was an M engraved on it. M for Maestro. But was it his?

Dashing out of the cabin, the Black Widow in the bath chair collided with the professor. Her veil slipped, and the professor thought he recognised her. But he was too dazed to tell me who it was. He had bumped his head hard. I helped him back to his cabin, neither of us realising that Wolf was already hiding in there, ready to strike! He knew the professor had recognised him, and so had murder in mind.

As soon as the cabin door was shut, Wolf killed the old man, strangling the professor with his own beard. I heard a thud, so I called out to the professor. From behind the cabin door, he replied that he was fine, but really it was Wolf putting on the professor's voice. Wolf isn't just a master of disguise – he is a master of accents too. This one was Hungarian.

MURDER WEAPON

A
BEARD

MURDER WEAPON

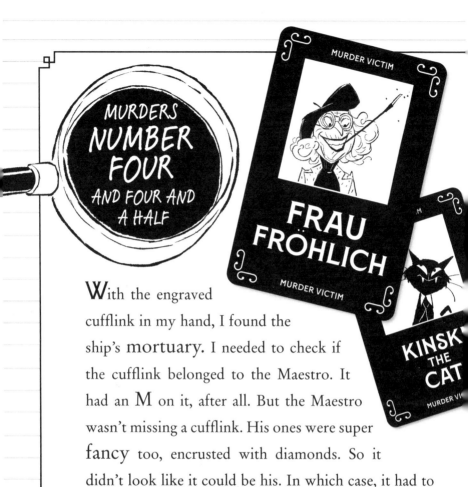

MURDER VICTIM

FRAU FRÖHLICH

MURDER VICTIM

KINSK THE CAT

MURDER VI

With the engraved cufflink in my hand, I found the ship's mortuary. I needed to check if the cufflink belonged to the Maestro. It had an M on it, after all. But the Maestro wasn't missing a cufflink. His ones were super fancy too, encrusted with diamonds. So it didn't look like it could be his. In which case, it had to belong to the murderer. Was the M for Morosov?

In the mortuary, the frozen chef was in the next drawer to the Maestro. But, deeper in the mortuary, there were more bodies hidden in the drawers.

One of them was alive!

Wolf had gone down there to hide the professor's body. But, when I disturbed him, he hid in a drawer.

When Watson sniffed him out, Wolf, still dressed as

the widow, and now out of her bathchair, went on the attack.

Watson and I just managed to escape. If we hadn't, we would have been murdered too.

My next stop was the captain's study. Sorry, Captain, but I broke in there to find out if the brigadier, Morosov or the Black Widow were on the passenger list. Of course, none of them were on the list because they were all being played by one man. That was my first inkling that these characters were all connected somehow.

Meanwhile, the captain had been sending telegrams all over the world asking for help as the bodies piled up.

Frau Fröhlich and her cat Kinski from Germany were the first to arrive. Frau Fröhlich craved the glory of unmasking the Maestro's killer, but soon she was found dead too – in the library, buried under a pile of murder-mystery books with her cat.

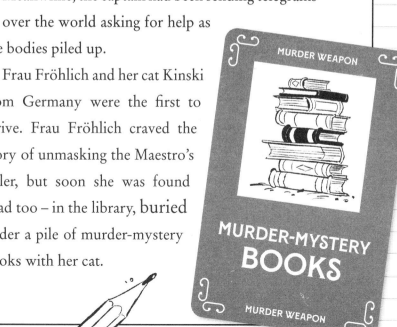

MURDER WEAPON

MURDER-MYSTERY BOOKS

MURDER WEAPON

Fröhlich must have been close to solving the case, which is why Wolf murdered her too.

This time, Wolf disguised himself as a blind composer named Magnus Magnus. Great name! But Wolf made a foolish mistake. He knew Fröhlich's cat was black. But, if he couldn't see, then how could he know?

MAGNUS MAGNUS

When I was discovered at the library, the scene of yet another crime, I was accused of murder!

So I was locked in the engine room, to be imprisoned there until we reached Southampton. But Wolf needed me to escape. I didn't realise it at the time, but it was so that more murders could be blamed on me.

That's why Wolf disguised himself as an engine-room worker and put on a perfect Scottish accent. This character, named Hunter, was one of his finest performances. Hunter freed me from the cell and persuaded me to disguise

HUNTER

myself to avoid capture. A disguise was something he knew would make me look as guilty as sin.

Once I had disguised myself as a waiter, Watson and I set about our detective work again. More of the captain's telegrams had been answered, and an embarrassment of famous detectives arrived. From England, Cyril and Cuthbert. From the Vatican, Sister Ruth. And from Egypt, Shariff. The chance to solve the murders of the Maestro and Frau Fröhlich was too great an opportunity for them to miss. If they cracked the case, they would earn their place in the history books.

Of course, all these famous detectives posed a deadly threat to Wolf. If they unmasked him, he would hang.

So, Wolf went on a killing spree!

MURDER
NUMBER
FIVE

MURDER VICTIM

SISTER
RUTH

MURDER VICTIM

MURDER WEAPON

GIANT
METAL WHEEL

MURDER WEAPON

Sister Ruth had hotfooted it to the engine room to interrogate me, the number-one suspect. However, Wolf flattened her with a giant metal wheel.

MURDER VICTIM

CYRIL

MURDER VICTIM

MURDER VICTIM

CUTHBERT

MURDER VICTIM

MURDER WEAPON

CHAMPAGNE BATH

MURDER WEAPON

Cyril and Cuthbert searched the Maestro's cabin. Wolf drowned them both in a bath full of their favourite drink, champagne.

MURDER VICTIM

SHARIFF

MURDER VICTIM

Meanwhile, Shariff had gone to the library to hunt for **clues.** This was, of course, the scene of Frau Fröhlich's murder. But there Wolf murdered Shariff by stuffing him into a giant glass bottle and replacing the cork. The poor man suffocated.

Because I was first to find his dead body, the maître d' pointed the finger of blame at me.

I was forced to go on the run from an angry mob. I desperately needed to find Fox. I trusted him. He was always so kind to me, even protesting my innocence. I

MURDER WEAPON

GIANT GLASS BOTTLE

MURDER WEAPON

thought he could help me. Protect me.

I hid from the mob in his cabin and spotted the faint outline of a W on his trunk. That's when I realised the M on the cufflink was an upside-down W. Stupidly, I had missed this! But immediately I knew that it wasn't an *M* I had been looking for all this time – it was a *W*.

W... for Wolf.

Hidden inside the trunk I found all the costumes he had worn for his characters: the brigadier, the Russian novelist, the Black Widow, the blind composer and the engine-room worker.

And that's not all: there were playbills from his many years in the theatre, newspaper cuttings of his crimes and a cache of murder weapons, including a scorpion in a jar!

Now it all made sense.

One man, in different disguises, had committed every single murder. "

Dilly pointed at Wolf.

"Ladies and gentlemen, MEET… THE LADY KILLER!"

In case anyone was in doubt, Watson pointed with his paw too.

"RUFF!"

CHAPTER THIRTY-FOUR

MURDER
NUMBER NINE

Wolf performed a slow hand clap.

CLAP! CLAP! CLAP!

"Congratulations, Little Miss Detective," he purred.

Gladys stared at him, shocked to the core.

"It's true?" she gasped.

Wolf bowed, and nodded.

"I can't believe I was about to become his next victim!" said Gladys.

"Oh! Please forgive me, my one true love," he purred.

"What about my diamond engagement ring?" she asked, displaying the giant rock on her finger.

Super Sleuth

"Worthless! Costume jewellery! A prop from one of my plays!"

"But...?"

"Tread on it!"

"What?"

"If it is a real diamond, it won't break."

Gladys tugged the ring off her finger and placed it on the floor. She stamped her foot on it...

STOMP!

...and the "diamond" crunched into a million tiny pieces.

KERUNK!

"Oh dear, oh dear," said Wolf with a smirk.

"So you're not rich?"

"No, I lost everything on the roulette tables of Europe, but as soon as I had murdered you I would have been."

Gladys ripped off his fake moustache...

"OUCH!"

... and slapped him hard across the face.

SLAP!

"That's for plotting to kill me!"

Then she slapped him harder.

SLAP!

"And that's for being poor!"

With all this slapping going on, the captain took charge.

"Thanks to brave little Miss Dilys here…"

"WOOF!"

"…and, of course, her dog detective, your murder spree is over. Max Wolf, I am placing you under arrest!"

"Can the condemned man enjoy one final drink?" he asked, raising a glass of champagne.

"I will grant you that," replied the captain.

"Then let me propose a toast, to the greatest actor-murderer the world has ever seen. Me!"

Dilly rolled her eyes.

Wolf took a sip of his champagne. He savoured the taste on his tongue and smiled. Then his face turned white, his eyes rolled to the back of his head and he collapsed.

Wolf dropped down... DEAD!

THE MURDERER HAD BEEN MURDERED!

CHAPTER THIRTY-FIVE

THE CONFESSION

Dilly leaped on to the stage.

"His lips are blue!"

Then she picked up his champagne glass. Flecks of red powder coated the inside.

"POISON!"

Panicked, Dilly looked up at her aunt.

"AUNTIE! DON'T DRINK THE CHAMPAGNE!"

"Don't worry! This one is fine!"

With that, the woman took a gulp.

"How do you know?" asked Dilly.

Gladys swallowed. "Um…"

Dilly stared at her, then at the glass and then at Wolf's glass.

She thought about her aunt's fury just now when she had learned Wolf was poor. An odd thing to be angry about, when he was a murderer! Then suddenly everything clicked.

"Auntie Gladys! You murdered Wolf!" exclaimed Dilly.

"Me? Don't be daft!" she replied, trying to act innocent. But, unlike Wolf, she wasn't much of an actor.

"Then why is he dead?"

"Is he?"

"YES!"

"RUFF!" agreed Watson.

"What in the blazes is going on?" demanded the captain.

"Nothing!" said Aunt Gladys. "Nothing at all!"

The captain took the champagne glass from Wolf's cold, dead hand. He sniffed the residue. "Rat poison."

"But it doesn't make sense," began Dilly. "Unless…"

"Unless what?" pressed the captain.

"Unless, Auntie Gladys, you were plotting all along to kill Lord Fox for his money, just as he was plotting to kill you."

"My goodness, you are good!" the captain interjected.

"No, no, no," spluttered Gladys. "I bet you poisoned him, Dilly! Out of hatred for me! Couldn't bear the

thought of me being happy! CAPTAIN! ARREST
HER!"

The captain was not stupid. He marched over to
Gladys and snatched her handbag. Searching inside, he
found a tin of rat poison.

"What's this, then?" he asked.

"I have never seen that before in my life!"

"It's rat poison."

"Oh yes! I remember! I had an infestation of rats in
my handbag, so…"

"I am placing you under arrest for the murder of Max
Wolf."

"Does it still count if you murder a murderer?"

"YES!"

"All right! All right! I confess! I killed him!"

"But why?" asked Dilly.

"For money."

"But, Auntie, you have oodles of money already."

"No. I don't have a penny."

"What?"

"There is no Great-Uncle Huw. I made him up!"

"So how did you afford all this? The trip to New York, the first-class cabins and all that expensive stuff you bought?"

"I used the money from selling the house."

"But that was my inheritance!"

"Yes! But I had to think about ME! So I splurged the lot on this trip. I needed the lord to believe I was rich too. Otherwise, he'd think I was just after him for his dosh."

"And you had to kill him a second after you were married?"

"I was gonna ask for him to be buried at sea, so…"

Dilly finished her aunt's sentence. "So that way no one would find out he had been poisoned."

"Yes. You clever little swine!"

"Why, thank you," replied Dilly sarcastically. "That's the nicest thing you have ever said about me."

"I loathe you. And I always did."

Dilly felt tears spring up in the corners of her eyes, but she blinked them back. This wasn't about her. This was about cracking the case.

"Well, Auntie," she said, her voice only breaking a tiny bit, "the wonderful thing is you are never going to have to see me again, as you are going to spend the rest of your life behind bars."

"CURSES!"

"Well done, Miss Dilys," said the captain. "You have caught not one but two murderers!"

"GRRR!"

"And, of course, you couldn't have done it without Watson."

"RUFF!"

Dilly patted her dog, smiling weakly.

"I suppose we'll never know how Wolf was planning to kill Gladys," mused the captain.

As everyone stopped to think, the ballroom went quiet.

Watson's super sensitive hearing picked up something. His ears twitched.

"What is it, Watson?" asked Dilly.

He dashed over to the wedding cake and pointed at it.
Dilly put her ear to it.

TICK! TOCK! TICK! TOCK!

"Captain?"

"Yes?"

"There is a bomb in this cake!"

CHAPTER THIRTY-SIX

CAKE BOMB!

"**A**AAHHH!" screamed the passengers as they fled from the ballroom, knocking over everything and everyone in their way.

BISH! BASH! BOSH!

"I'm glad I poisoned the rotter!" shouted Gladys as she too fled the scene.

"This bomb could blow a hole in the ship!" exclaimed the captain. "Then we are all done for."

"RUFF!" agreed Watson.

"Let's hurl it into the ocean!" said Dilly.

TICK! TOCK! TICK! TOCK!

"No, Miss Dilys. You and Watson run to the lifeboats. You have your whole life ahead of you!"

The captain rushed over to the cake and began wheeling it out of the ballroom.

"It's faster with two!" exclaimed Dilly.

"WOOF!"

"I mean three!"

"RUFF!"

Watson pushed with his head, and together they whizzed off.

TICK! TOCK! TICK! TOCK!

The gangways were awash with panicked passengers, reeling from side to side in the storm.

"HELP!"

"OUT OF THE WAY!" cried Dilly.

"CAKE BOMB COMING THROUGH!"

added the captain.

This only made the passengers panic more.

"NOOOOOO!"

Young and old leaped aside, as the explosive cake sped towards the staircase.

SHUNT!

The wheels of the trolley hit the bottom step, and the cake slid forward.

"NO!" cried the captain.

TICK! TOCK! TICK! TOCK!

Thinking fast, Dilly pushed down hard on the end of the trolley, and the cake slid back towards them.

298

The captain caught it just in time.

TICK! TOCK! TICK! TOCK!

"Phew!" he said.

"RUFF!" agreed Watson.

"How are we going to get it up the stairs?" asked Dilly.

"You go to the front. See if we can lift it."

But it was too heavy.

TICK! TOCK! TICK! TOCK!

As more passengers rushed past, the captain cried, "HELP! WE NEED TO GET THIS CAKE BOMB UP THE STAIRS!"

Instead of helping, the passengers ran for their lives!

"AAAHHH!"

"Oh dear," said Dilly.

Then she looked down. "Where's Watson?"

Turning round, she saw the dog dragging the maître d' along by his trouser leg.

"SHOO! SHOO!" he shouted.

But Watson was not giving up! Using all his strength, the plucky little fellow yanked the man closer and closer to the trolley.

TICK! TOCK! TICK! TOCK!

Watson yanked so hard on the maître d's trousers that they ripped…

RRRIIIIIIP!

…and flew off!

WHOOSH!

"I HAVE NO *PANTALONS*!" he cried.

"I DON'T CARE ABOUT YOUR *PANTALONS*!" shouted the captain. "YOU NEED TO HELP US OR THE WHOLE SHIP IS GOING TO BLOW!"

"I would love to help, *Capitaine*, but I am *très* busy right now!"

"Doing what?"

"Leaping over the side!"

"HELP US, YOU *IDIOTE*!"

The maître d' muttered something in French, then ran round to the front of the trolley. He and Dilly just managed to lift the wheels off the ground as the sturdy captain took a greater share of the weight at the back.

Together, they lifted the trolley up the staircase, as **THE MASQUERADE** bounced off the waves.

TICK! TOCK! TICK! TOCK!

However, just as they reached the final step, DISASTER STRUCK!

Gladys was fleeing, laden with bags and boxes of all the nonsense she had bought in New York. The tower of boxes was so tall she couldn't see where she was going. She collided with the maître d'.

DOOF!

He lost his grip on the trolley.

"*NON!*"

And, as it spun, the captain lost his grip too.

"NOOOOOOO!"

Only Dilly was still holding on.

She and the trolley bounced down the staircase, her legs in the air.

BUMP! BUMP! BUMP!

"AH!" she cried.

"WOOF!" barked Watson, but there was nothing anyone could do right now. The trolley with the cake bomb was so heavy, and travelling so fast, that it would kill anyone in its path.

BUMP! BUMP! BUMP!

Then, as soon as it hit the bottom, it would

EXPLODE!

CHAPTER THIRTY-SEVEN

KABOOM!

As everyone looked on, helpless to stop the inevitable, Watson raced down the staircase, before leaping ahead of the speeding trolley.

"WOOF!"

"WATSON! NO!" cried Dilly.

Then he jumped up on to the shelf at the bottom of the trolley.

One by one he pushed down on the locks on the wheels with his nose.

CLICK! CLICK! CLICK!

Still the trolley was tumbling down the staircase.

BUMP! BUMP! BUMP!

CLICK!

Watson hit the final lock, and the trolley lurched to a halt.

Such was the force of the stop that the cake bomb bounced off the trolley up into the air.

WHOOSH!

Any second now, it would hit the floor and...

KABOOM!

With her foot, Dilly flicked the locks back off the wheels.

CLICK! CLICK! CLICK!

She shoved the trolley forward...

SWUSH!

...and the cake bomb landed safely on it.

"PHEW!" she exclaimed.

But now the cake bomb was back at the bottom of the stairs. There was no time to lose.

TICK! TOCK! TICK! TOCK!

"COME ON!" she cried.

The captain and the trouser-free maître d' hurled themselves down the staircase.

Instantly, the team went back to work. In seconds, they had the trolley at the top of the staircase, and out on to the deck.

Passengers were leaping into lifeboats.

TICK! TOCK! TICK! TOCK!

The crew was helping them.

TICK! TOCK! TICK! TOCK!

But the storm was deadly!

TICK! TOCK! TICK! TOCK!

The sea would take them!

TICK! TOCK! TICK! TOCK!

And the cake bomb was still on board!

TICK! TOCK! TICK! TOCK!

ANY MOMENT NOW THE CAKE BOMB WAS GOING TO EXPLODE.

"To the bow!" ordered the captain.

As fast as they could, they powered the trolley to the front of the ship.

SWOOSH!

But, looking over the side, Dilly saw there was a lifeboat **jam-packed** with **passengers** rocking on the waves.

"PORT!"

TICK! TOCK! TICK! TOCK!

But there they spotted a whale

swimming alongside the ship!

BLUB! BLUB! BLUB!

"STARBOARD!"

TICK! TOCK! TICK! TOCK!

No! A family of **puffins** was

frolicking there!

"SQUAWK! SQUAWK! SQUAWK!"

"STERN!"

TICK! TOCK! TICK! TOCK!

This was their final hope.

The trolley sped along the deck.

SWOOSH!

The maître d' ran out of puff and

collapsed on the deck.

"GO! GO! GO!" he cried.

Then Dilly tripped over someone's umbrella and fell.

"CAPTAIN!" she shouted.

But still he and Watson kept going.

SWOOSH!

The trolley hit the back of the ship hard.

DOOF!

The cake bomb was sent flying and then…

KABOOM!

It **exploded** in mid-air.

The captain was hurled
backwards by the force of the blast.

His lifeless body hit the deck.

THWUMP!

"NOOOOOOOOOOOO!"

cried Dilly.

CHAPTER THIRTY-EIGHT

TRAGEDY AND COMEDY

A hail of cake, cream and icing pelted the ship.

SPLATT! SPLUTT! SPLOTT!

The captain's body was covered in what was left of the wedding cake.

He had saved the lives of everyone on his ship.

But he had paid a terrible price.

"CAPTAIN!" Dilly cried, rushing to him.

But she couldn't hear him breathing, and when she searched for a pulse on his neck, she couldn't feel one.

"NOOOOOOOOOOOOOOO!" she screamed at the sky.

She cradled his head in her hands, tears streaming down her face.

Then she heard a gurgle.

"BLEURGH!"

Looking down, she saw the captain spit some cake out of his mouth.

"This cake is revolting," he exclaimed.

"YOU'RE ALIVE!"

"I believe so, Miss Dilys," he said, checking his arms and legs. "And everything is shipshape."

She helped him to his feet, just as the maître d' caught up with them. A crowd was forming, all jostling to catch a glimpse of the cake-covered captain.

He looked like the Abominable Cakeman.

CAKE-COVERED CAPTAIN

THE ABOMINABLE CAKEMAN

"THREE CHEERS FOR THE CAPTAIN!" said Dilly. "HE SAVED US ALL! HIP! HIP!"

"HOORAY!"

"HIP! HIP!"

"HOORAY!"

"HIP! HIP!"

"HOORAY!"

Everyone broke into wild applause.

CLAP! CLAP! CLAP!

"PLEASE!" cried the humble captain, wiping cream from his eye. "It is not me you should be cheering. It is this young lady here. This super sleuth solved the murders, put her life in danger time and time again, and saved us all. MISS DILYS IS THE REAL HERO!"

Even wilder cheers and applause greeted her. Dilly glowed red with embarrassment, though she felt a surge of pride too.

"But," she began, "I couldn't have done any of it without the help of my faithful assistant, Watson!"

"**RUFF!**" he agreed, standing on his back legs and performing a little dance to delight the crowd.

After all the tragedy, now there was comedy.

Just like the two masks.

"HA! HA! HA!"

"THANK YOU!"

"I AM SORRY FOR THE WHOLE DRAMA ABOUT THE SHOE!"

Dilly reached out her arms and Watson leaped into them. He licked her face just a little too much.

"SLURP! SLURP! SLURP!"

"Steady on, Watson!"

Again, there were cheers from the crowd.

"WATSON'S A HERO!"

"Give that dog a medal!"

"And a dog biscuit!"

"RUFF!" he agreed.

The captain put his arm round the girl, and said, quite simply, "Thank you."

Soon, the storm had passed, and **THE MASQUERADE** had docked safely in Southampton.

The passengers and crew all disembarked, leaving just Dilly and the captain on board.

She watched from the bow as her wicked aunt was handcuffed and bundled into the back of a police van.

Gladys glared out of the window. She gave her niece one final grimace, and then she was gone.

BRUMM!

"So, Miss Dilys," began the captain, "who should I call to collect you?"

"I don't know," she replied. "I don't have any family. No home. And nowhere to go. It's the orphanage for me." She swallowed. She was terrified of the orphanage, but what could she do? And, anyway, there was somebody who mattered more. "What about Watson, though?" she asked.

"RUFF!"

"What about Watson?"

"They would never let me bring my dog. He would end up in a pound. Promise you will look after him for me, Captain? Please?"

"RUFF?"

"Of course," said the captain.

"Thank you! You're the best!"

"But what about you? Surely you don't want to go and live in an orphanage?"

Dilly shrugged, biting her lip. "I don't have any choice. I never have."

"What if you did have a choice?"

"I don't understand," said Dilly.

"Well," said the captain kindly, "if you wanted, Miss Dilys, I could look after you too…"

A huge smile spread across her face.

"YES!" she exclaimed.

IT WAS A GIANT YES!

She wrapped her arms round him and didn't ever want to let go.

"RUFF!" barked Watson as he nuzzled against the captain's leg.

"Oh! And," said the captain, a tear rolling down his cheek, "I might just have a little job for you both…"

EPILOGUE

Indeed, he did.

"Miss Dilys, how would you like to live on board THE MASQUERADE?" asked the captain.

"YES, PLEASE!"

"RUFF!"

"We will sail around the world."

"Marvellous!"

"And I will put you both in a lovely cabin!"

"You're the best!" exclaimed Dilly.

"All I ask of you is one thing…"

"Name it!"

"I want you two to be the ship's onboard detective team, looking out for crimes, keeping an eye on any suspicious goings-on."

"That would be a dream come true!"

"RUFF!"

"Splendid!" said the captain. "And you can have banana milkshakes for breakfast, lunch and dinner!"

"YES!"

"WOOF!"

"And Watson can have all the dog biscuits he can eat!" added the captain.

"RUFF!"

That's exactly what happened.

The captain even had a sign made, which was placed on their cabin door.

In big black letters it proclaimed:

THE MASQUERADE departed Southampton, bound for adventure. Dilly even penned her own casebook.

All the detective duo needed now was another murder.

Or two.

Or three.

Or four.

Or more…!

THE END?